$7.60

Kor

Korman, Susan
Hector's haunted house.

DATE DUE

NO 3 '99		
DE 7 '99		
JA 5 '00		
NO 11 02		
JUN 6 '03		
AP 14 08		

An Unwelcome Guest

Hector spotted a plain white envelope without a postmark. The letter was addressed to THE CARRERO FAMILY. Curious, Hector ripped it open. Inside was a sheet of white paper with jagged edges, as if it had been torn from a notebook.

"What's this?" Hector started to say. But the words stuck in his throat as he read the message scrawled on the page.

> Dear Maritza and Hector,
>
> Beware! Your new house at 101 Ellington Street is haunted! A ghost roams through the house at all hours, and it does not like strangers living in its home. . . .
>
> A Friend

JOIN THE TEAM

Do you watch GHOSTWRITER on TV? Then you know that when you read and write to solve a mystery or unravel a puzzle, you're using the same smarts and skills the Ghostwriter Team uses.

We hope you'll join the team and read along to help solve the mysterious and puzzling goings-on in all of the GHOSTWRITER books!

HECTOR'S
HAUNTED HOUSE

by
Susan Korman

Bantam Books
New York   Toronto   London   Sydney   Auckland

HECTOR'S HAUNTED HOUSE
A Bantam Book / September 1997

Ghostwriter is a registered trademark of Children's Television Workshop.
Ghostwriter™ and ● are trademarks of Children's Television Workshop.

Cover design by Marietta Anastassatos.

The money that Children's Television Workshop earns when you buy
Ghostwriter books is put right back into CTW educational projects.
Thanks for helping!

ISBN 0-553-48480-X

Published simultaneously in the United States and Canada.

Bantam Books are published by Bantam Books, a division of Bantam
Doubleday Dell Publishing Group, Inc. Its trademark, consisting of the
words "Bantam Books" and the portrayal of a rooster, is Registered in U.S.
Patent and Trademark Office and in other countries. Marca Registrada.
Bantam Books, 1540 Broadway, New York, New York 10036.

PRINTED IN THE UNITED STATES OF AMERICA

OPM   0 9 8 7 6 5 4 3 2 1

For Kevin, Connor, and Jack,
the members of *my* home

CHAPTER 1

"There it is, Uncle Ruben!" nine-year-old Hector Carrero shouted as his uncle turned down Ellington Street. Hector pointed to one of the buildings in a row of brick homes. "That's our new house, number one-oh-one!"

"I know, Hector." Uncle Ruben laughed as he slowed down and scanned the street for a parking space. "I've been here a million times already helping your mother with repairs."

"I don't know who's more excited about our new house," Hector's mother, Maritza, chimed in, "me or Hector!"

"I'd say it's a tie," Ruben declared. He maneuvered the van into a spot along the curb. "But it's not every day you buy your own house."

As soon as his uncle had shut off the engine, Hector opened the door and took off for the steps in front of 101 Ellington Street.

Hector's new house was a narrow, two-story brick building. White paint was peeling off the shutters, and the steps out front were starting to crumble, but Hector and his mom had lots of plans for fixing things up. Maritza had already put a pot of colorful pansies near the front door, and Hector noticed that the house looked more inviting.

Hector stared at the upstairs window on the right. That was his new room, and he couldn't wait to get settled in. For the past few years, Hector had lived with his mom in a small apartment. Now they would have tons of space.

Hector tried the front door.

"It's locked, Hector," his mother called out. "Please come back over here," she added with a smile. "The van is filled with our stuff. Nobody is going into that house empty-handed!"

"Okay, okay," Hector said. As he headed back to the van he saw a group of six kids coming toward him.

Hector started waving madly. "Hey, you guys!" he yelled. "You're just in time. We haven't unloaded a single thing yet."

"Shucks!" Thirteen-year-old Jamal Jenkins groaned as he ran a hand through his dark hair. "We were hoping we'd get here *after* you guys moved all the stuff in."

"Don't worry, Jamal," Maritza said. "My friends from work brought the real heavy stuff over last night. We just need help unloading the things we packed this morning."

"No problem, Ms. Carrero," Alex Fernandez said, flexing his muscles. "With this kind of strength, I can lift *anything*."

"Give me a break, Alex!" His younger sister, Gaby, rolled her eyes. "That's not what I heard you saying to Dad this morning when he asked you to carry stuff into the *bodega*."

Alex turned beet red while the others laughed.

"Well, we appreciate any help we can get," Ruben broke in. He swung open the van's back doors. "Grab whatever you can."

Tina Nguyen reached for a lamp while Gaby and Jamal each took a box marked TOOLS.

"You can put the tools downstairs," Maritza said. Maritza worked as a carpenter, and she planned to set up a wood shop in the basement.

As Hector stood waiting for his uncle to give him something to carry, he noticed Ruben handing Alex a big cardboard box. Before Alex could take it, Hector jumped in front of him.

"Whoa!" Surprised, Alex stepped backward. "What's in that thing, Hector?" he asked. "Or is it top secret?"

Hector flushed. "Uh . . . my baseball posters," he told Alex. "And my autographed Roberto Clemente baseball card. It's pretty valuable. I wanted to make sure nothing happened to this stuff during the move."

Hector's grandfather had given him the baseball card, and Hector had been collecting posters of Latino baseball players since he was seven. He had decided to decorate the walls of his new room with the baseball stuff. Before Alex could make fun of him, he grabbed the box and headed up the walkway.

Inside the house, Maritza was giving Gaby a quick tour of the bottom floor.

"Isn't it great?" Hector said proudly.

"It sure is," Gaby agreed. "You guys even have a little backyard."

"And it's all ours," Maritza said.

"Your mom's really proud, isn't she?" Gaby whispered to Hector as Maritza started toward the kitchen.

Hector nodded. "This is her dream come true," he said.

Hector's parents had separated before he was born, so it had always been just Hector and his mom. Maritza had been talking about buying a house for as long as Hector could remember. As soon as she'd seen the house at 101 Ellington Street, she'd decided it was perfect for the two of them.

Gaby followed Maritza into the kitchen while Hector ran upstairs with his baseball stuff. His new room had a wooden floor and two large windows. It wasn't a big room, but his mother had given the walls a fresh coat of paint, and everything looked neat and clean.

Hector dropped the box on the floor and glanced at the blank walls. For a minute, he was tempted to hang up a few of his posters, but then he remembered that his friends were all downstairs, working hard. Decorating his new room would have to wait.

By late afternoon, the van was almost empty.

"We're nearly finished," Ruben called, disappearing into the back of the van. "Except for . . ." He came back, carrying a large wall mirror with a cobalt blue frame. "This."

"Hector and I can carry that," Jamal volunteered.

"Please be careful with that mirror, guys," Maritza called from the house. "My friend Sylvia made that for a housewarming present, and I don't want anything to happen to it."

"No problem, Mom," Hector said. "You've got an expert moving team here."

"I sure do," Maritza said. She gestured to the rest of Hector's friends. "Come on inside for a cold lemonade, everybody."

Ruben handed down the mirror. Hector took one end, and Jamal grabbed the other. Carefully the two started for the front door.

"So do you know anything about the people who used to live in your house?" Jamal asked.

Hector shook his head. "It was empty for a long time before we bought it. My mom said that's why the price was so low," he added. "The guy who used to own it was desperate to sell. He accepted Mom's first offer."

"That's cool," Jamal said.

When they reached the steps that led up to the house, Hector turned around and started up backward.

"Watch out, Hector," Jamal called as Hector began guiding the mirror through the narrow doorway. "This thing is pretty big. I'm not sure it's going to fit."

Hector glanced over his shoulder. "I think it's okay," he started to say. "If you—"

Just then the sound of a voice startled him.

"Hellooooooo."

As Hector whirled around to see who was there, the mirror slammed into the door frame.

Crash!

Hector watched in horror as the mirror shattered. Splinters of glass flew everywhere.

"Oh, man." Jamal was still holding on to the frame. "I can't believe this!"

"What a shame," someone said.

Hector looked up. A woman stood on the walkway in front of his house. She was heavyset, in her fifties, with a pale complexion and blue eyes. She wore a white uniform, including an apron, and there were traces of white powder in her hair and on her forehead. She held a white box labeled LYON'S BAKERY.

"Oh, boy," the woman went on, clucking her tongue. "A broken mirror on your first day in a new house is a terrible omen."

CHAPTER 2

"A terrible omen?" Jamal repeated.

The strange woman nodded.

"That's just a stupid superstition," Hector snapped. "A broken mirror doesn't mean bad luck." He stood glaring at her until she held out a hand. "I'm Marion Wolf," she said. "Your new next-door neighbor."

"Oh." Hector felt his anger fade a little as he shook her hand. "I'm Hector Carrero. My mother and I just moved in."

Marion's large white teeth flashed as she smiled. "No need to introduce yourself, Hector. I know all about you and your mom."

"You do?"

8

Just then Hector's mother hurried over. "Are you two okay? I heard glass breaking. . . ." Her voice trailed off as she saw the broken mirror at Hector and Jamal's feet. "Oh, no," she said softly.

"I'm so sorry, Mom," Hector said. "It was an accident."

"I saw the whole thing," Marion Wolf piped up loudly. "What a shame—on your first day in the new house, too."

Maritza looked startled. "It's okay," she said quickly.

While Marion introduced herself to Maritza, Hector went to get a broom and dustpan. When he returned Marion was thrusting the bakery box into his mother's hands. "Just a little something to welcome you to the neighborhood," she said. "My son, Brent, and I live over there." Marion pointed to the house on the left.

Hector glanced over at the house. It was almost identical to his, except for the blue paint on the shutters and the blinds that hung in all the downstairs windows. Upstairs, he noticed, a dark shade was pulled down.

"You have a son?" Maritza said.

"That's right, but you won't see much of him, except maybe at night," Marion said, beaming.

"He's a college student and he has a part-time job over at the BSM. When he's not studying, he's working. In fact"—Marion lowered her voice and leaned in closer to Maritza—"his computer-science professor thinks he's quite gifted. Maybe even a computer *genius.*"

"That's wonderful," Hector's mother started to say. "You must be very—"

"I don't know what I'd do without Brent," Marion interrupted. She heaved a sigh. "Since my husband died six years ago, Brent's the only family I have."

Maritza nodded sympathetically. "He must be quite a boy."

"He is, and I . . ."

Hector handed the dustpan to Jamal, trying to tune Marion out as they started to sweep up the shattered glass.

"What a motormouth," Jamal whispered.

Hector nodded. He had the feeling that Marion would talk all day if his mother didn't find a way to stop her.

Hector was sweeping the last bit of glass into the dustpan when something Marion said caught his attention again.

"Yes, siree. My husband and I lived in your

house for nearly twenty years—right up until he died."

Hector stared at Marion, surprised. She had lived at 101 Ellington Street, too?

"A few months after my husband died, I was forced to sell the place. I didn't want to, but I just couldn't keep up the mortgage payments."

"What a shame," Maritza replied.

Hector saw Marion shrug. "You gotta do what you gotta do," she said. "Luckily, like I tell Brent all the time, at least we were able to rent the house next door and stay in the neighborhood. That's where we've been living since the sale."

"Well, it's been very nice to meet you," Maritza said, holding out her hand.

Way to go, Mom, Hector thought. His mother was about to make her escape.

Hector glanced at Marion, waiting for her to take the cue. But Marion paid no attention to Maritza's hand. Instead she was looking past his mother, as if she were trying to steal a glimpse inside the house.

"I'd better get back inside," Maritza said.

"Oh." Marion looked startled, but this time she saw Maritza's hand and she took it. "My pleasure. I'm glad our house is occupied again. Frankly," she added, "the last owner didn't take very good care of *our* home." With that, Marion waggled her fingers, then left for the house next door.

Hector followed his mother into the kitchen.

"I can't stand that lady," he fumed, sitting down at the table with his friends.

"Who?" twelve-year-old Lenni Frazier asked, sipping a tall glass of lemonade.

"My new neighbor," Hector complained. He told them about how the mirror had broken. "It's that lady's fault. She scared me to death."

"She likes to talk, that's for sure," Jamal put in. "And it was a little weird how she kept calling this 'our house,' like she still lived here."

"Now Hector . . ." Maritza placed the white bakery box on the table and cut the string with a knife. "Marion might be a little annoying, but she's trying to be friendly. And she's our next-door neighbor. I don't want any trouble with her."

"She's not a *little* annoying, Mom," Hector said. "She's *really* annoying. Plus she's nosy. Didn't you see her trying to peek inside at our stuff?"

"No," Maritza said firmly. "And look . . ." She peered into the box. "She even brought over your favorite cookies—chocolate chip."

"I don't care," Hector said. "She's—" Before he could finish, someone burst into the kitchen.

"Yoo-hoo!" Marion sang out.

"Doesn't she know how to knock?" Hector muttered under his breath.

Across the table, Gaby giggled.

"Silly me!" Marion said, slapping herself on the side of her head. "I was so excited about meeting my new neighbors, I completely forgot the most important thing. . . ." She dumped a stack of letters on the table. "I've been keeping your mail for you."

She's been keeping our mail? Hector thought. *Why?* As far as he knew, his mom hadn't asked Marion to do that.

"My goodness," Marion said as she gazed around at the kitchen. "My husband chose the color for this room. I'd forgotten how lovely this shade of green is."

Lovely? Hector and his mother hated the pea-green walls. One of the first things they wanted to do was paint the kitchen white.

Hector scowled as his mother thanked Marion and walked her to the front door.

"You're right, Hector," Tina said when Marion was out of earshot. "Your new neighbor does like to talk."

"Yeah. And I think she's nosy, too," Casey Austin said. Casey was Jamal's eight-year-old cousin.

"She was looking around at all your stuff. I wonder if she was snooping through your mail, too."

"Who cares if she's nosy?" Alex said. He bit into a cookie. "These are the best chocolate-chip cookies I've ever tasted!" He held out the box. "Try one, Hector. They're great."

"Okay," Hector grumbled. He took a cookie, trying to ignore the fact that it had come from Marion, then started flipping through the stack of mail.

Most of the letters looked pretty boring—like junk mail. *Mom definitely won't be happy to see these,* Hector thought, setting aside a few bills. Then, at the bottom of the stack, Hector spotted a plain white envelope without a postmark. The letter was addressed to THE CARRERO FAMILY.

Curious, Hector ripped it open. Inside was a sheet of white paper with jagged edges, as if it had been torn from a notebook.

"What's this?" Hector started to say. But the words stuck in his throat as he read the message scrawled on the page.

> Dear Maritza and Hector,
> Beware! Your new house at 101
> Ellington Street is haunted! A

*ghost roams through the house at
all hours, and it does not like
strangers living in its
home. . . .*

                              A Friend

CHAPTER 3

As he reread the note, Hector's fingers trembled and he could feel his heart pumping furiously.

Beware! Your new house at 101 Ellington Street is haunted!

"What's up, Hector?" Jamal asked.

Lenni chuckled. "You look like you've seen a ghost!"

Numbly, Hector handed the note to Jamal.

Jamal scanned the letter. "Check it out!" he said, smiling. "Hector's new house is haunted!"

"What?" Casey grabbed the paper out of Jamal's hand. She read the note aloud, then started to laugh. "The note is signed, 'A Friend.' I bet Ghostwriter is playing a joke on you, Hector!"

"No way!" Hector shook his head. "Ghostwriter

would never write a note like this one—even as a joke."

Ghostwriter was an invisible friend who communicated with Hector and his friends only through reading and writing. After Ghostwriter had contacted each one of them, they had formed the Ghostwriter team. They'd become close friends and had even solved several mysteries together—with Ghostwriter's help.

"I agree," Lenni chimed in. "Ghostwriter wouldn't do something like this. It must be somebody else's idea of a joke."

"But whose?" Gaby said. She turned to Hector. "Do you know any of your neighbors?"

"Only one," he replied. "Remember?"

Gaby rolled her eyes. "How could I forget Marion Wolf?"

Hector shoved the note into his pocket as his mother walked back into the room. She was so happy today; he didn't want anything to upset her, especially since he'd already broken her mirror.

But Hector was still worrying about the note when he walked his friends to the door a few minutes later.

Gaby patted his shoulder. "Forget about it, Hector. Your new house is great—and it *isn't* haunted."

"Right," Alex put in. "That note is just a stupid joke."

"See?" Gaby said, smiling. "It's got to be true—how often do Alex and I agree on something?"

Hector smiled. He tried to tell himself that his friends were right—the note was just a dumb joke. He wasn't going to let it spook him anymore.

Hector spent the next few hours helping his mother unpack boxes and put away dishes in the kitchen. At dinnertime, she handed him a ten-dollar bill from her wallet.

"I haven't had time to go grocery shopping," she said. "Could you run out and get us some sandwiches from the deli on the corner?"

"Sounds good to me," Hector agreed.

By the time he'd returned with the food, his mother had set out paper plates and paper cups, and she'd tuned the radio to Hector's favorite station.

"This almost feels like home," Hector said, pulling two sandwiches and a bottle of soda out of the bag.

"Almost," his mother said. "Although it's not really home until you're all settled in."

Hector unwrapped his sandwich and smiled.

"I'm going to that deli all the time," he said. "The man gave me extra pickles."

Maritza smiled back. "He certainly knows how to get my son to come back to his store!"

As they ate, Hector's mother talked about her plans for the new house. "Once we get the wood shop set up in the basement, you can finish the bench you've been working on."

Hector nodded. His mother had started teaching him how to make things out of wood when he was little. Now he was old enough to use most of her tools. Last year Hector had made a bookcase on his own, and his latest woodworking project was a bench for their new backyard.

"I can't wait to tear down the wallpaper in the dining room," Maritza went on. "It must be at least twenty years old." She made a face at Hector. "Did you get a look at those big red flowers?"

"Yup. Pretty gruesome," Hector agreed.

"Maybe we can paint the walls beige, or a really pale . . ."

Hector didn't hear the rest of his mother's sentence. As she was talking, the lights in the kitchen flickered. Then, abruptly, the music died and the room went black.

"That's strange," Hector said with alarm in his voice.

"It sure is." Maritza stood up. "We'd better look at the circuit box downstairs," she said, frowning.

There was just enough light from the streetlights outside for Maritza to dig through one of the boxes in the living room for a flashlight. Then Hector followed her down the creaky steps into the pitch-black basement.

Relax, Hector told himself. *The power just went out. That's all.*

But all Hector could think about was the note tucked in his pocket: *Beware! Your new house at 101 Ellington Street is haunted!*

What if the ghost had turned out the lights? A shiver traveled up Hector's spine.

The basement was a big, musty room with several tiny, cracked windows that looked out onto a paved alleyway and a door that opened out into the backyard. The room was empty except for a few stacks of boxes and some wood piled under a long, low table.

Hector brushed aside cobwebs as his mother opened the circuit box and trained the flashlight on two columns of switches.

"That's odd," she said.

"What's odd?" Hector asked quickly.

His mother frowned. "The main circuit breaker has been thrown."

"What does that mean?" Hector asked.

"The main circuit breaker controls all the electricity in the house," Maritza explained. "For some reason, the switch tripped. That's only supposed to happen if there's a dangerous surge of power, like when you're using too many appliances."

"But we only had on the lights and the radio," Hector pointed out. "That's not a lot of electricity."

His mother nodded. "I hope there's nothing wrong with the electrical wiring," she said in a worried tone. "There shouldn't be a problem— Leticia just redid all the wiring."

Maritza flipped the black switch at the top of the two columns. Hector was relieved when he heard the radio in the kitchen come back on.

"I don't get it." His mother shrugged. "I'll ask Leticia to come back to look things over, but I can't imagine why the power would go out so suddenly like that."

Hector could imagine one reason: *Maybe the ghost did it!* he thought.

As soon as they got back upstairs, Hector reached for the phone to call Alex and Gaby.

"We won't have phone service until tomorrow," his mother reminded him. "But I'm sure Marion Wolf wouldn't mind if you used her phone."

Hector made a face as he hung up the receiver.

His mother laughed. "She doesn't bite, you know."

"She's too busy *talking* to bite anybody," Hector mumbled. "I guess I will borrow her phone," he added.

Hector grabbed his jacket. Before he left for Marion's house, his mother gave him a hug. "Thanks for all your help today, honey. It's going to take a while to fix everything up, but the important thing is that we're here together."

"Yeah." Hector forced a smile. He didn't want to tell his mother, but he wished they were back in their old apartment.

It was small, Hector thought. But at least it didn't have ghosts.

CHAPTER 4

As Hector walked over to Marion Wolf's house, he saw a car with an enormous plastic pizza on top zoom away from the curb.

Marion stood at the door shaking her head. "I can't believe this," she said to Hector. "That's the third time tonight those rotten kids had a pizza delivered to my house." She glared at him. "I hope you don't start hanging around with those two troublemakers."

"What troublemakers?" Hector asked.

"Xavier and Miles." Marion made a disgusted face as she waved a hand toward the other end of the block. "They live up the street, and their idea of a good time is giving me a *bad* time. Last week they had five tubs of Cluck-Cluck fried chicken sent to my house. The week before, it was thirty dollars' worth of Chinese food!"

"That's not very nice," Hector mumbled.

"You bet it's not very nice," Marion shot back. "But those two think nothing's funnier than playing a practical joke on a poor widow like me. They're two of the . . ."

"Uh, Mrs. Wolf," Hector said. "Would it be okay if I used your phone?"

"Of course you can use the phone," Marion said, opening the door and letting him inside. She gave a little chuckle. "Unless you're planning to call someone overseas."

"Nope." Hector shook his head. "Just some friends who live in Fort Greene, too."

"Well, in that case . . ." Marion led Hector through the living room into the kitchen. There was clutter everywhere. Dusty magazines were piled on the floor, and laundry was scattered all over the couch and coffee table. A tall young man with Marion's pale skin but dark eyes and hair sat on the couch staring at a TV set. He didn't look up until Marion spoke to him.

"Brent, this is Hector. The boy who moved in next door."

Brent glanced at Hector and grunted.

"I know you're busy with your studies," Marion

24

said to Brent as she rolled her eyes at Hector, "but I'd really appreciate it if you could get this laundry folded and put away before I leave for work. I'm not a one-man show, you know. I . . ."

Hector bit back a smile as Brent gave his mother a bored look. Having Marion as your mom couldn't be easy, Hector thought.

"Right this way, Hector," Marion said. They headed into the kitchen, which was just as messy as the rest of the house.

"The phone's right there," Marion said, pointing to the wall. "I'll be upstairs getting ready for work. I've got the graveyard shift tonight."

"The graveyard shift?" Hector asked. "What's that?"

"Most nights I work from midnight to six in the morning," Marion explained. "I'm a baker at Lyon's Bakery." She let out a heavy sigh. "Baking sticky buns and frying crullers all night long sounds like a fun job, but it's not. First you gotta . . ."

For the next five minutes Marion told Hector more than he wanted to know about twisting dough into crullers. Finally Hector managed to break in. "Can I use your phone now, Mrs. Wolf? My mom's expecting me home soon."

"Why didn't you just say so?" Marion looked

bewildered. Hector was relieved when she finally left the room. Quickly he dialed Gaby and Alex's phone number.

"Hello?" Alex picked up right away.

Speaking softly so Marion wouldn't overhear, Hector told him how the electricity at his new house had mysteriously gone out. "Do you think my house really is haunted?" he asked worriedly.

"Hector . . ." Alex laughed. "Don't tell me you really believe a ghost is playing games with your electricity!"

"I'm not sure, Alex. But even my mom thought it was weird. Especially since her friend Leticia re-wired the whole house right before we moved in." Then Hector blurted out what was really worrying him. "It happened just as my mom was telling me about all the changes she wants to make in the house."

"So?"

"So remember what that note said—about the ghost thinking the house belongs to it? Maybe the ghost doesn't like strangers changing everything around."

"That's crazy, Hector," Alex said. "You've got to forget about this note. Moving is a big deal," he went on. "Maybe you're just freaking out about leaving your old apartment."

"I miss the apartment a little," Hector admitted. "But I—"

"Tell you what," Alex cut in. "Let's treat this like a case that we're trying to solve. We'll get the team together tomorrow after school. We can even start a casebook."

"That sounds good," Hector said. He felt relieved as he hung up the phone. Alex was right. He would feel better if his friends could help him figure out who had sent that spooky note.

A half hour later, Hector and his mother headed up the stairs for bed. As Hector opened the door to his room, he groaned. He'd completely forgotten about the unpacked boxes sitting on the floor. "I can't believe how much work there is when you move to a new place," he complained.

His mother nodded. "You look tired, honey," she said. "And tomorrow's a school day. Why don't you just unpack your clothes. The rest can wait."

Hector stifled a yawn. "Just don't tell my friends I went to bed at eight-thirty, okay?"

"It's a deal," his mother said with a grin.

Before leaving the room, Maritza went over to the tall mahogany dresser that stood against the far wall. "You can put your clothes in here," she said.

"Roberto, the man who lived here before us, left it behind. It's a nice piece."

Hector shrugged, too tired to care about an old piece of furniture.

"Good night, honey." Maritza kissed him on the forehead. "Fold your clothes neatly, okay?" she added on her way out.

As soon as his mother was out of sight, Hector grabbed the box containing his clothes and started dumping everything into the dresser drawers as fast as he could.

As Hector opened the bottom drawer, something caught his eye. A starched white handkerchief sat on top of an old newspaper, which was folded open to the real-estate section. Reaching in to scoop them out, his fingers touched something else—a crumpled-up old photograph of a family standing in front of a brick house.

Nobody will miss this stuff, Hector decided, and he tossed the picture, along with the paper and handkerchief, into the trash.

Then he quickly shoved his clothes into the last empty drawer. "Presto!" he said and wiped his hands clean. He'd managed to finish unpacking in five minutes flat.

Hector put on a pair of pajamas and was about to climb into bed when he heard kids' voices drifting in from outside. He went over to the window that looked out on the alleyway between his house and the Wolfs'. Over on the next street, he could see a small park, where some kids were playing basketball under the lights. Nearby two teenage boys wearing New York Mets baseball caps were skateboarding along the paved path, doing all kinds of fancy moves.

What a cool view of the neighborhood, Hector thought. From his window, he could see Ellington Street *and* check out the action in the park. He could see the deli on the corner, where the nice man had given him the extra pickles. And a few blocks away, he could see a large, three-story building—the science museum.

The only bad thing about this view, Hector decided, was that it was right opposite a window in Marion Wolf's house. He hoped Marion wouldn't try to spy on him.

Looking back toward the other end of Ellington Street, Hector noticed something else. It was a small, cleared-out area between two row houses, closed off by a chain-link fence. *Maybe it's another park,* Hector thought. He decided to check it out on his way home from school the next day.

Yawning again, Hector climbed into bed. He noticed his mother had put out his favorite old flannel comforter. Hector couldn't help feeling glad to have something familiar in his strange, new room.

He turned off the light and felt how heavy his eyelids were. He couldn't remember when he'd been so tired. . . .

Hector was almost asleep when he felt a presence in his room. "Mom?" he muttered sleepily as he rolled over to look.

But when Hector opened his eyes, he didn't see his mother—he saw an eerie, white light hovering in the darkness.

CHAPTER 5

Hector gasped and bolted up in bed. He rubbed his eyes, but the white light still shimmered in the room.

Then, abruptly, the light disappeared.

Hector sat rigid in bed, nervously scanning the dark room. He could hear his mother unpacking and moving things around in the next room. But he couldn't stop thinking about the strange light, and where it had come from.

He got out of bed and went to the front window. The street was deserted, but there was plenty of light—neon signs glowing in the distance, and the yellow glare of streetlamps along the curb.

Maybe the white light was some kind of reflection, Hector thought. He climbed back into bed.

It was a long time before Hector fell asleep. And when he finally did doze off, images of shimmering ghosts swirling over his bed haunted his dreams.

The next afternoon Hector sat on the stoop in front of his house, waiting for the rest of the team to arrive.

A voice jolted him to attention. "Are you Hector?"

Two boys wearing blue Mets baseball caps were standing in front of him, skateboards under their arms.

"That's me," Hector said, nodding.

"I'm X," the taller boy said. He had a handsome face and closely shaved hair, and wore baggy shorts with a huge T-shirt printed with the letters *BSM*. X nodded to his friend. "This is Miles."

Miles was short and stocky. His eyes were hidden by a pair of dark sunglasses. As Hector looked at the boys, he realized they were the two teenagers he'd seen skateboarding in the park the night before. "Your name is X?" Hector said to the tall boy.

X nodded. "That's right."

"It's short for Xavier," Miles explained.

As they repeated their names, something else dawned on Hector: These were the "troublemakers" Marion had been complaining about. These were the kids who'd had the pizzas and the fried chicken delivered to her house.

"So how long are *you* going to be living here?" X asked.

Hector shrugged. "My mom says forever. Why?"

The two boys exchanged glances.

"Oh yeah?" A sly grin slid across Miles' face. "I guess your mom likes haunted houses or something."

"What?" Hector felt his stomach clench.

"One-oh-one is haunted, man," X said.

"That's right," Miles chimed in. "Roberto, the guy who lived there before you, told us about all kinds of weird stuff happening. He said the electricity would go off, stuff would be missing. He even heard a ghost moaning one night."

"What?" Hector said again.

X shook his head. "I guess you didn't hear about the guy who was murdered there either," he added.

"Murdered?" Hector's mouth was so dry, he croaked out the word.

"Yeah. I'm not sure when it happened," X went

on. "All I know is that the guy's ghost still roams around the house, leaving a trail of blood."

"Did you sleep there last night?" Miles asked, looking at Hector with concern.

Hector nodded slowly.

The boys exchanged glances again.

Then X dropped his skateboard and hopped on. "I wouldn't worry about it too much if I were you, Hector," he said. "As far as we know, nobody's been murdered there in a while."

"Yeah . . ." Miles indicated the house next door with his eyes. "All you have to worry about is 'the Wolf' huffing and puffing and blowing your house down!"

Both X and Miles burst out laughing.

Then, before Hector could say anything, the two took off skateboarding down the street. Neither one looked back.

Hector sat there, stunned, as if he'd been punched hard in the stomach. A man had been murdered in his house? And now the man's ghost roamed around, doing weird things like shutting off the electricity?

Mom and I made a big mistake, Hector thought. *An enormous mistake. We never should have bought this house.*

"Hector?" Lenni said. "Are you okay?"

Hector was so worried, he hadn't even noticed his friends arrive. "No. I'm not okay." He told the team what X and Miles had just told him.

"I've seen those two jokers around," Jamal said. "They're always playing tricks on people, Hector. I bet they made up those stories."

Lenni agreed. "Didn't your neighbor say they were troublemakers, too?"

"But . . ." Hector told his friends about the electricity going off the night before, and the strange light he'd seen in his room. "What if what they're saying is true? What if it really is a ghost?"

Alex smiled. "I think you're just still getting used to the house, Hector."

"Maybe," Hector said slowly.

"Come on," Tina said. "Let's start a casebook, like Alex suggested. The only way to help you relax, Hector, is to find out what's really going on."

"Okay," Hector agreed. He went into the house and returned a moment later with a notebook. He opened it to a clean page and labeled it EVIDENCE. He labeled the next page SUSPECTS.

"Okay," Gaby started, "so what's our evidence?"

"The note," Hector said. "And the electricity going out."

He wrote those things down.

"The white light you saw in your room is evidence, too," Casey said. "And so are X and Miles' stories."

"Yeah," Lenni said dryly, "evidence that those two are liars."

"What about suspects?" Tina asked. "Do we have any?"

"Yup." Hector wrote "Ghost!" under the Suspects heading.

"Hector." Gaby shook her head. "That's what we've been trying to tell you. "There is no such thing as a . . ."

Just then a glowing green light started dancing across the page. As it moved, it picked up letters and swirled them into a message:

Did someone mention a ghost?

"Ha!" Hector turned to Gaby with a triumphant look. "Who says there's no such thing as a ghost?"

"Hi, Ghostwriter!" Hector wrote.

Hello, everyone, Ghostwriter replied. The swirling light quickly traveled across the page again

36

as Ghostwriter read the casebook. Hmmm . . .
So your new house is haunted, Hector?

"Yes," Hector wrote.

Then Gaby leaned over with her pen. She
crossed out the "Yes" and wrote *"No!"* beneath it.
"Someone just wants Hector to *THINK* the house
is haunted, Ghostwriter," Gaby wrote.

Oh. Well, I must admit that I find the pos-
sibility of meeting a real ghost very interesting. . . .

Jamal laughed softly. "It sounds like Ghostwriter
is hoping to bump into another ghost."

Hector felt irritated. *Maybe Ghostwriter wants to
meet a real ghost,* Hector thought, *but I don't.*

"Ghostwriter, this is serious," Hector wrote.
"Can you help us find any evidence of a real
ghost?"

I'd be delighted to try, Ghostwriter replied.

Tina nudged Hector. "Ask him to search your
room," she said. "That's where you saw the light
last night."

"The basement, too," Jamal added. "Ask Ghostwriter to look near the circuit box for clues."

Hector wrote down his friends' suggestions. A second later, the glow faded as Ghostwriter took off to search Hector's house.

While they waited, Lenni added X and Miles to the Suspects page.

"I'm *sure* they wrote the note," she said. "It's their idiotic way of welcoming you to the neighborhood, Hector."

Hector shrugged. He hoped Lenni was right, but he still wasn't sure.

A few minutes later, a glowing light flashed across the page. Ghostwriter was back. The first thing he spelled out was a date.

" 'September 19, 1982,' " Alex read aloud.

"Hey, look," Jamal said. "He found some addresses, too. They're streets in Brooklyn, I think."

Hector nodded as the letters grew clearer. Written under the date were three addresses:

    12 Lincoln Street
    138 Sullivan Avenue
    413 Third Street

Then Ghostwriter started writing something else.

"See, Hector!" Lenni exclaimed as the clue grew brighter. "I told you that those two had something to do with this!"

As Hector stared at the notebook, his eyes widened. Glowing brightly in the middle of the page was a single letter:

X

CHAPTER 6

Before Hector's friends went home, they promised to meet him the next day after school to start investigating the clues Ghostwriter had found. After they were gone, Hector wandered aimlessly around his new house. He didn't feel like unpacking the boxes in his room or hanging up his baseball posters. When he tried to do his homework, he couldn't concentrate. All he could think about were X and Miles and the stories they had told him.

After dinner, Hector's mother suggested going for a walk. Hector jumped at the chance to get out of the house for a while. He followed his mother out into the warm spring air and locked the door behind him.

"Good evening, you two," said a loud voice. It was Marion Wolf.

"Oh, great," Hector groaned softly. "Now we'll get stuck here all night."

His mother shot him a warning look. "Hi, Marion," Maritza said in a friendly tone. "Are you heading out to work?"

Hector saw that Marion was dressed in her bakery uniform.

"Don't remind me," Marion complained. "My back is killing me already. I must have baked ten dozen sticky buns last night."

"It must be tough working the graveyard shift," Maritza said.

"You've got no idea." Marion shook her head. Hector thought she was going to continue complaining, but suddenly she frowned and changed the subject. "By the way, Hector, I saw you talking to those two troublemakers this afternoon."

"Those are my friends," Hector began. "They're not—"

"Not them," Marion said, scowling. "Xavier and Miles. Those boys are nothing but trouble," she went on. "In fact, this afternoon, while I was trying to take a nap, the two of them called me up and asked for 'wear.'"

"Wear?" Hector repeated.

"That's right," Marion snapped. "As in *were*-wolf? Have you ever heard of anything so . . ."

Hector quickly ducked down and pretended to tie his sneaker. He didn't want Marion to see him smiling. X and Miles might be troublemakers, just like Marion said, but Hector thought they were also pretty funny.

When Hector stood up again Marion was muttering something about forgetting her watch. Hector heaved a sigh of relief when she headed back into her house. He and his mother continued on down Ellington Street.

"Boy, she complains a lot," Hector remarked.

"She's had a hard life, Hector," his mother said. "In the last six years, she's lost her husband and her home."

"Well, if she stopped grumbling all the time, maybe things would get better," he said.

"It's not easy raising a son and holding down a job, you know," Maritza replied.

Hector didn't say anything, but he wanted to point out to his mother that she was doing the same thing, and she didn't complain.

As they reached the corner, Hector noticed the small, cleared-out area he'd seen last night from his window. Tonight the chain-link gate was open, and two women holding rakes stood inside. Nearby were several mounds of soil and a big, red wheelbarrow.

"A garden!" Maritza exclaimed.

"Cool," Hector said. He read the plaque attached to the fence: ELLINGTON STREET COMMUNITY GARDEN.

As Hector and his mother stood outside the fence looking in, the two women came over and introduced themselves. Hector liked them immediately; he could tell that his mom did, too.

"Are you two in charge of the garden?" Maritza asked the woman named Barbara.

"Not really," she said. "Everybody on Ellington pitches in to help."

"How does it work?" Hector asked.

"There are twenty plots available to the residents of Ellington Street," the other woman, Sue, explained. "People sign up pretty quickly, but this year, we've got one plot left." She smiled. "It could be yours—if you're interested in growing vegetables or flowers."

"Sign us up, Mom," Hector said, elbowing his mother gently. "We can grow watermelons."

Maritza signed their names on the sheet of paper

that Sue handed her. "Thank you. Having a garden will be so wonderful."

Hector and his mother chatted with the women for a few more minutes.

"Barbara and I are pretty handy," Sue said after Maritza told them about the repairs she'd started making on their new house. "We'd be glad to help out."

Hector's mother took the women's phone number and promised to call them. Hector realized how happy he was that his mother had made some new friends. Barbara and Sue were really nice, and they seemed a lot more fun to hang out with than Marion Wolf!

As Hector and his mother started down the block again, Hector heard Barbara call out two names.

"X and Miles! Get over here and give us a hand."

Hector turned around and saw X and Miles riding their bikes up Ellington Street toward the garden.

"Oh no, you don't," Sue said cheerfully as the two boys started to turn their bikes around. "Come on, you guys. We're waiting."

"Oh, man!" Reluctantly, X got off his bike and walked it over to the garden.

Miles followed. "I just finished helping my mom wash the dishes," he complained.

"We just need some help spreading this soil around," Barbara told them. "It'll only take a few minutes."

X and Miles continued to grumble, but they picked up shovels and started to help.

"Are those boys the 'troublemakers' Marion was talking about?" Maritza asked.

Hector nodded.

"They look like pretty nice boys to me," said Maritza.

"I guess," Hector said. He and the rest of the team were planning to talk to X and Miles tomorrow. Maybe then he'd find out just how nice they really were.

As Hector and his mother continued their walk around the neighborhood, Hector pointed out the science museum he'd seen from his window. When they passed the deli where Hector had gotten sandwiches the day before, the deli clerk, José, came out.

"It's pickle boy!" he said to Hector.

Hector laughed. "They were really good pickles. Thanks again."

A short while later, Hector and his mother started back toward their house. "I'm glad we moved to Ellington Street," Maritza said. "The people are so nice, and I love the idea of the whole block working together to create a community garden. Just think, Hector," she went on, "this summer we can grow our own herbs and tomatoes and string beans. . . ."

"No way, Mom," Hector cut in. "We are definitely *not* growing string beans. They're totally disgusting."

His mother laughed. "Okay, no string beans," she promised.

As they walked along, Hector noticed that the sun had set, and the sky had turned midnight blue. *Mom's right,* he thought suddenly. *This is a nice street. I'd probably like living here—if I didn't have to worry that my house was haunted.*

Hector followed his mother up the walkway in front of their home.

"How about zinnias?" she asked, putting her key in the lock and pushing open the door. "They're such colorful flowers, and they look so pretty when . . ."

As Maritza stepped into the hallway, she gasped.

"What is it, Mom?" Hector demanded. He pushed past her, without waiting for a reply.

Hector stopped short. Spattered all over the beige carpeting in the entrance hall were dark red droplets.

Blood! Hector thought, and shivered. *It looks like a trail of dried blood!*

CHAPTER 7

Hector's knees wobbled as he stepped closer to the trail of blood. He bent down to get a closer look.

"I can't believe this," his mother said, crouching next to him. "The drops still look wet."

"Still wet?" Hector echoed.

It was a warm night, but an ice-cold shiver went through Hector again. He remembered X's words: "The guy's ghost still roams around the house, leaving a trail of blood."

Slowly Hector stood up. The color had drained out of his face. He turned to his mother to tell her what X and Miles had said. But he noticed she was looking up at the ceiling. "What are you doing, Mom?"

"The bathroom is up there," she murmured. "We must have a leak."

"A leak? But these drops don't look like water, they look like—"

"The pipes are old and rusty," his mother interrupted. "I was hoping we wouldn't have to replace them for another few years," she went on with a sigh. "Maybe I'll call Leticia. She's coming over tomorrow to look at the electricity—she can look at the plumbing then, too."

As his mother hurried off to use the phone, Hector's eyes flicked back and forth between the ceiling and the rust-colored drops staining the carpet.

Mom's right, he thought. *It's just water—rusty water from a leak.*

But Hector couldn't stop his panicked thoughts. What if it really *was* a trail of blood left by the ghost? What if the ghost came back later—when Hector and his mother were sleeping? What if the ghost really was some murdered guy who . . .

"You okay, Hector?" his mother asked, coming back into the room. "You look a little pale."

Hector forced himself to nod. "I'm fine. Do you really think it's a leak, Mom?" he asked.

"Of course it's a leak," his mother said, giving him a curious look. "What else could it be?"

"Uh . . ." Hector faltered. He didn't want his mom to know what he was really worried about.

Suddenly her expression changed. "Oh, honey . . ." Maritza said. "*I* got you all worried, didn't I? I'm sorry I overreacted about the pipes. I promise, once we've been here awhile, I won't panic about every little thing that goes wrong with the house."

Hector nodded, then hugged his mother. He wished it were only a leak in the pipes he was worried about.

In his room, Hector tried to study for the history quiz he had the next day. But there was no way he could concentrate on ancient Egypt after finding what looked like a trail of dried blood in his house.

Hector put down his textbooks and reached for the team's casebook. He opened it and read the clues they'd gathered so far:

Evidence
note that says "Beware of ghost"
electricity going out
white light in Hector's bedroom
X and Miles' stories about a ghost
September 19, 1982

The last clues on this list were the three addresses that Ghostwriter had found, and the big X. Picking up his pen, Hector added the newest evidence to the list: "trail of blood on the carpet." A second later he wrote a question mark next to the words. Maybe his mother was right, and the "blood" really was rusty water.

Hector turned the page and read the Suspects list.

Suspects
Ghost!
X and Miles

Hector realized that he'd been so worried about his house being haunted by a real ghost, he hadn't considered the other suspects very carefully.

X and Miles did have a motive, he thought. They liked to play jokes on people. And Ghostwriter had found that X somewhere in Hector's house.

Then Hector realized something else. Earlier in the night, he had seen X and Miles riding their bikes away from Hector's house.

Could they have gotten in and spilled "blood" on the carpet? Hector wondered. It seemed like a lot of effort for a dumb joke, but maybe they'd somehow managed to pull it off.

Suddenly the words on the page began to flicker.

Good evening, Hector.

Hector reached for his pen again. "Hi, Ghostwriter! Boy, am I glad to see you."

Because I'm such delightful company? Ghostwriter wrote back.

Hector chuckled. "Sorry, Ghostwriter, but that's not exactly why I'm so happy you're here. I'm still worried there's a ghost in my house."

Of course there's a ghost in your house! Ghostwriter answered.

Hector blinked in surprise. Did Ghostwriter think that the house was haunted, too?

The words on the page began to swirl again.

Tee hee! Remember me—your friend, the ghost?

"Very funny, Ghostwriter! You scared me!"

I'm sorry, Hector. I couldn't resist a little joke. But seriously, I want to help you find this ghost.

"Why?" Hector wrote curiously.

Because it's scaring you, Ghostwriter wrote. And . . . He seemed to hesitate for a second. Well, sometimes it gets a little lonely being the only ghost around here, he added. Then abruptly he changed the subject. Let's see what you have so far.

Hector couldn't help feeling relieved as he watched Ghostwriter zip across the casebook, reading the lists of clues and suspects.

It does seem as though something suspicious is going on, Ghostwriter wrote when he had finished. This could be evidence of a ghost, but . . . Ghostwriter paused.

"But what?" Hector prodded him.

I'm afraid that ghosts aren't the only ones who haunt houses.

Hector was confused. "What do you mean, Ghostwriter?"

Sometimes people's hearts linger in a place long after they've moved away. You can feel their presence even though they're not there themselves.

"Huh?" Hector said aloud. He had no idea what Ghostwriter was talking about.

Hector watched Ghostwriter take off and zip around the stack of unpacked boxes and rolled-up posters sitting in the middle of Hector's room.

I'll help you track down your ghost, Ghostwriter wrote when he returned. But in the meantime, I have a suggestion.

Hector picked up his pen. "What is it, Ghostwriter?"

Finish unpacking, Hector. Settle in and make this your true home. Maybe that will chase your ghost away.

"Rats," Hector mumbled as Ghostwriter faded away. Ghostwriter hadn't been much help at all.

For the next few minutes, Hector just stared at

the casebook, thinking about what Ghostwriter had said about people's hearts lingering in a place long after they'd moved away.

It made Hector wonder about the family who'd moved into his old apartment. Could they sense his presence, as well as his mother's? Could they tell that he liked baseball and was good at solving mysteries?

What a strange idea, Hector thought, smiling a little.

As he closed the casebook, Hector remembered how Ghostwriter had said it was lonely being the only ghost around. Hector had never realized that Ghostwriter could get lonely, too.

Just then Hector's mother knocked on the door. "Hector? I hope you're studying for that history quiz in there."

"Uh . . . I've got it covered, Mom," he fumbled.

"Good."

As his mother walked away, Hector reluctantly reached for his history book again. He didn't feel like studying, but he knew he'd better get started. His teacher's quizzes could be even more frightening than a haunted house.

CHAPTER 8

The next day Hector stood at the corner of Ellington Street after school, waiting for the team to meet him. They were going to start investigating the clues that Ghostwriter had found.

"What took you guys so long?" Hector demanded when the team finally showed up.

"Hector," Gaby said patiently. "We're only five minutes late."

"You've got to stop stressing about this ghost," Lenni added, patting him on the shoulder.

"You don't know what happened last night," Hector retorted. He filled in his friends about the blood-colored stains on the carpet and how he'd seen X and Miles coming up the street on their bikes.

"Are you saying they could have dripped fake blood on your rug?" Lenni asked suspiciously.

"Maybe," Hector said. "Although they would have had to break into our house to do it. And there were no signs of a break-in."

A sly grin crossed Alex's face. "Ghosts can travel through walls, you know," he said in a spooky voice.

Hector made a face. "Cut it out, Alex."

"Someone could enter your house through that basement door," Casey said. "Did you check that out?"

Hector shook his head. "I know that door was locked, too," he said firmly. "My mom's really careful about stuff like that."

"If we want to track down the ghost, we should check out those three addresses Ghostwriter found," Jamal reminded everybody. He pointed to the nearby subway station. "Come on. Let's go."

Twenty minutes later the team stood in front of the first address: 12 Lincoln Street.

It was a blue, single-family house with a small patch of overgrown grass out front.

Hector rang the doorbell.

A balding man wearing shorts and a Yankees

sweatshirt came to the door. He peered at the team through thick glasses. "Can I help you?"

Casey elbowed Hector.

"Er . . ." Hector didn't have the slightest idea how to explain what they were doing on this man's doorstep. "Excuse me, sir," he fumbled. "Do you know anything about a house on Ellington Street?"

"Number one-oh-one Ellington Street," Alex added.

The man scratched his head. "I'm not sure I even know where that is. Why?"

Hector hesitated.

"We're trying to learn more about the neighborhood for a school project," Alex said quickly.

"Oh," the man said. "That sounds interesting, but I'm afraid I can't help you. I've only lived here for two or three months. Before that I lived in the Bronx."

"The Bronx?" Jamal repeated.

"That's right. And boy, do I miss it. I could walk over to Yankee Stadium." He stared at the team. "Are any of you baseball fans?"

"I like the Yankees," Hector said politely. "But the reason we're here, sir—"

"I think those Yankees have a shot at another pennant this year—don't you?" the man cut in.

As Hector stood there listening to the man talk

about the Yankees, he couldn't help thinking that this guy liked to talk almost as much as Marion Wolf did. If the two of them ever got together, forget about it!

Finally Jamal managed to interrupt. "Thanks for your help, sir. We have to get going."

"Nice meeting you," Hector added. Then he and his friends turned and raced down the steps before the man could get in another word.

"Too bad he didn't have anything to say about Hector's house," Alex said.

"So where do we go next?" Casey asked.

Hector consulted the casebook. "One-thirty-eight Sullivan Avenue," he replied. "That's just a few blocks away."

A few minutes later they knocked on the door of a brick house at 138 Sullivan Avenue.

"It doesn't look like anyone's home," Alex said, trying to peer past the sheer white curtains in the windows.

Gaby knocked a few more times, but no one came to the door.

Hector noticed several letters addressed to R. Garcia sticking out of the mailbox. "Nobody's taken in the mail yet," he told his friends. "Maybe these people are still at work or something."

Jamal nodded. "Let's check out the third address. If we don't find out anything there, we can come back here later."

As the team turned up the walkway in front of 413 Third Street, Hector saw an elderly woman sitting outside on a lawn chair in front of the four-story, brownstone building.

Jamal introduced the team and asked the woman if she knew anything about 101 Ellington Street. "It's for a school project," Hector quickly explained.

The woman told them her name was Flora Tyson and she'd been living in this house her whole life. "I was born here eighty years ago and have no intention of going anywhere until I die," she said.

"Wow," Hector said. He was amazed that the woman had lived in the same place for so many years.

"I bet you've seen a lot of changes on this block since you were a kid," Lenni said politely.

"I sure have." Ms. Tyson nodded. "I can remember the days when nobody had automobiles. Trolley cars used to ride up and down this block, and we took them everywhere."

Hector gazed around, trying to imagine how the street looked eighty years ago. As he glanced back toward the house, it suddenly struck him that it was a big place for just one lady.

"Ms. Tyson, do you rent out part of your house?" Hector asked.

"I sure do," Ms. Tyson said. "A very nice young couple just moved in upstairs. They've been here for about two months, since the end of March."

Gaby and Hector exchanged looks.

"Would you mind asking them if they know anything about one-oh-one Ellington Street?" Gaby asked.

"Not at all," Ms. Tyson said. "But they moved here from Long Island. They don't know much about Fort Greene or about the rest of Brooklyn."

The team chatted with Ms. Tyson for a few more minutes. Before they left, Hector gave her his phone number, in case her tenants knew anything about his house.

On their way to the subway, the team stopped again at 138 Sullivan Avenue, but the house still looked dark and empty.

Hector sighed as the team trudged down the subway steps. "We're never going to figure out this case," he muttered.

"Sure we will," Gaby said, trying to cheer him up. "We just started the investigation. You should know by now, Hector, solving mysteries takes time and patience."

"It's hard to be patient when you think your house is haunted," Hector grumbled.

Lenni quickly changed the subject. "Isn't it amazing that Ms. Tyson has lived in the same house her whole life?" she said. "I can't imagine still living in my apartment when I'm in my eighties!"

"Me neither," Alex chimed in. "I like living in Brooklyn and everything, but I want to travel and see more of the world."

"I don't want to move around a lot," Casey said abruptly.

They all looked at Casey, surprised.

"Why not, Casey?" asked Tina.

"I think it would be nice to live in the same house for your whole life," Casey said. "It's important to feel like you have a home. That's how Ms. Tyson must feel about her house."

Hector was still thinking about what Casey had said about having a home when the team's train pulled into the station. He definitely didn't feel that way about his house yet. It was a place to live—but it wasn't a home.

"Well, look who it is," Jamal muttered as the team turned down Ellington Street a little while later.

Hector glanced up. Skateboarding on the sidewalk in front of his stoop were X and Miles.

Lenni picked up her pace. "Good. I have some questions for those two," she said.

X looked startled when he saw the team approaching. "What's up, Hector?"

"Not much," Hector replied. He introduced the team to X and Miles.

"You're the kids who warned Hector about his house being haunted, right?" Lenni said.

"That's right," Miles said. "We thought he should know about it."

"Do you guys know anything about the trail of dried blood that Hector and his mother found last night?" Alex asked.

"Blood?" X's eyes went wide. "Oh, man," he breathed. "You found it too, Hector? Just like the guy who used to live here?"

Hector nodded.

Miles shook his head. "I guess Roberto *was* telling the truth about those moans he used to hear and that ghost roaming around. You'd better be careful, buddy," he added.

"I agree," Lenni said, pretending to go along. "It's pretty scary stuff. You guys seem to know so much about the neighborhood," she went on, "I was wondering if you knew anything about this date. . . ." She looked at the casebook to find the clue that Ghostwriter had brought them. "September 19, 1982."

"Why are you asking?" Miles asked.

Lenni lowered her voice. "The ghost wrote that date on a piece of paper in Hector's room," she lied.

"Really?" Miles adjusted his baseball cap as his eyes slowly traveled to X. Hector saw a look pass between them. "Now that you mention it," Miles went on slowly, "I might know something about that date. I think it might have been when that guy was murdered at one-oh-one."

"Yeah," X joined in. He pointed to one of the upstairs windows at Hector's house. "I think it happened right up there."

Hector couldn't help it. He let out a loud gasp. X was pointing right at his bedroom window!

CHAPTER 9

"What?" Jamal stared at X and Miles in disbelief.

Even Lenni stopped pretending to go along with the two boys. "No way," she said. "I don't believe that somebody was actually murdered in Hector's bedroom."

Miles' lips formed into a sly smile. "You don't *have* to believe it. . . ." he said softly.

A shiver went through Hector. *I believe it!* he thought.

"Do you know any more details?" Gaby asked. "Like who was killed, and who did it?"

"Nope." X shook his head. "All we know is that it happened, and—"

"There was a lot of blood," Miles cut in.

"A *real* lot of blood," X emphasized. "Even though most of it had dried up by the time the police got there."

In his head, Hector was picturing the dark red drops on his carpet.

"So what were you guys doing near Hector's house just now?" Alex changed the subject.

For a second neither boy answered.

"What is this?" Miles said finally. "A police interrogation or something?"

"No," Jamal said, folding his arms. "We're just wondering why you're hanging out here, and not at the park or something."

"We were . . . uh . . ." Finally X took a deep breath. "The Wolf called our parents about all the jokes we've been playing on her," he blurted out. "They made us come over to apologize."

"So you were hanging out at Hector's because you didn't want to go over to Mrs. Wolf's?" Gaby asked.

X nodded.

Alex laughed out loud. "Don't tell me you two are actually afraid of the big bad Wolf!"

"We didn't say we were *afraid*. We said we were stalling," Miles retorted.

"Come on." X hopped off his board. "Let's do

it right now, Miles. If our parents need witnesses, these kids will stand up for us."

Hector watched the two boys head up the stairs in front of Marion's house. They rang the bell, and a second later Marion's son opened the door.

"They're actually doing it," Tina muttered as the boys disappeared inside the house. "I didn't believe them, but it looks like they're actually going to apologize to Marion Wolf."

"Those two are too much," Lenni said, shaking her head.

"I'm sure nobody was murdered at your house, Hector," Jamal said. "Didn't Marion live here before that guy, Roberto, sold it to your mother?"

Hector nodded. Then something occurred to him. "Maybe it was Marion's husband who was murdered."

"I don't think so," Jamal said. "I heard her tell your mother that her husband died suddenly of something else. Plus Marion said he died six years ago. September 19, 1982, is *fifteen* years ago."

Hector nodded, reassured.

"Maybe X and Miles lied about apologizing to

Marion, too," Gaby said. "Just because they went inside the house, it doesn't mean they're actually apologizing."

"That's true," Lenni agreed. "I think they're liars with a capital *L*."

Hector pulled out his key and unlocked his own front door.

He glanced around nervously, checking to see if everything looked okay inside the house. To his relief, there were no signs that anyone—ghosts included—had visited in his absence.

He showed the team where he and his mother had found the trail of rust-colored stains the night before. "My mom cleaned it up so you can't see it anymore, but it was right here," he said, pointing.

"It must be a leaky pipe," Jamal said, looking up toward the ceiling. "See? The paint's peeling up there—probably from the moisture. When your mom's friend comes over later to look at the plumbing, you'll know for sure."

Hector nodded. Everything his friends had been saying made sense. Maybe the ghost's "blood" really was just rusty water, and the "ghost" itself really was just two neighborhood kids playing a stupid practical joke.

"I'm starving," Casey said suddenly. "How about a snack, Hector?"

Everybody laughed at her bluntness.

"Sure." Hector led the team into the kitchen. Luckily his mom had gone grocery shopping. He held up a bag of pretzels.

"Perfect," Casey declared.

They all sat at the kitchen table. Lenni asked Hector for the casebook. She munched on a pretzel as she reviewed the case.

Alex pointed to the X under the list of clues. "What we have to do," he said, "is find out where Ghostwriter found this X."

"Right." Lenni rubbed her hands gleefully. "Then we can prove once and for all that X and Miles are the ghost."

Hector picked up a pen and wrote a note to Ghostwriter. A moment later, a sparkling light swept across the page.

Hi, Team.

Hector circled the X under Evidence. "Ghostwriter, we're trying to figure out where this came from. Can you try to read something near it?"

Sure. Ghostwriter vanished, then returned in a minute.

"He found something," Casey announced.

Hector held his breath as Ghostwriter gathered letters from the page. He spelled out the word *tools*. Then he began writing something else.

"Those look like book titles—history books," Jamal commented.

Hector read the titles aloud: *"The Life of Martin Luther King, Jr.; The Great War;* and *Benazir Bhutto: An Intimate Portrait."*

"I don't own any of those books," Hector said. "And neither does my mom. I hope Ghostwriter finds another clue."

Ghostwriter disappeared again.

A moment later he spelled out something else on the page:

BSM . . .

Hector frowned as Ghostwriter wrote the letters again and again.

BSM . . . BSM . . . BSM.

"What's that?" Tina mumbled.

"I know I've seen those letters before," Alex said, scratching his head.

"Me, too," said Hector. But he couldn't remember where.

✒ Attention, Reader! Do you remember where Hector has seen the clue, BSM . . . BSM . . . BSM?

—Ghostwriter

CHAPTER 10

An hour later, Hector walked his friends to the door. "I wish I could remember where I've seen those letters before," he sighed.

Jamal nodded. "I bet it will come to one of us, Hector. In the meantime," he added, "why don't we try to track down that guy who used to own your house?"

"That's a good idea," Hector agreed. "My mom told me he still lives in Fort Greene. Maybe he knows something else about the ghost."

"Or he can tell us if those stories are even true," Lenni chimed in.

"We can visit him on Saturday," Tina said. "After we go back to that address where no one was home—138 Sullivan Avenue."

When everyone had left, Hector paced up and down the living room.

"If you're bored, Hector," his mother said, "I can think of plenty of things for you to do. Like finish unpacking the boxes in your room," she said.

Hector shook his head. For some reason he didn't feel like putting away the stuff in his room. "Maybe I'll go downstairs and work on the bench I'm making," he said.

"Good idea." His mother nodded her approval. "You're almost finished. The wood shop's all set up," she added as he opened the door that led to the basement.

Hector flicked on the lights and started down the rickety wooden steps.

It was late afternoon, and barely any light came in through the tiny, cracked windows near the ceiling. The darkness and chilly air made him think of an abandoned dungeon.

Hector crossed the room to the work table, where his mother had set up her shop. The wood he was using for the bench lay on the floor. As Hector bent down to lift one of the long strips, he felt something brush his fingers.

"What was that?" he gasped. A second later he saw a big spider skittering across the floor.

"Chill out, Hector," he told himself. He took a deep breath, then bent down again to pick up the wood.

Hector placed the wood on the table, then reached inside a gray metal box for a tape measure. Suddenly, a word printed on the side of the box jumped out at him: TOOLS.

Hector froze. That was one of the clues that Ghostwriter had brought the team earlier that afternoon. Hector and the team had been so distracted by the clue "*BSM . . . BSM . . . BSM,*" that they'd forgotten about the other clues.

Quickly Hector glanced around. Maybe Ghostwriter found all the clues—the book titles, the *X,* and the *BSM*—down here, he reasoned.

Cautiously Hector stepped away from the workbench. Remembering how the electricity had gone out the other night, he walked over to the circuit box, and opened the door. Carefully he checked to see if there was an *X* or a *BSM* inside. But he didn't spot either clue.

Hector wandered through the rest of the room. Near the door that led outside was a small area the size of a closet, where the oil tank stood. Hector examined the fat, barrel-shaped tank. On the floor underneath the tank's legs he noticed a cardboard box.

"What's this?" Hector said aloud. He reached under and dragged the carton closer. It was old and mildewed, and looked like it had been there for a long time. Hector saw that the box was filled with books. Hector read the title of the book on the top of the pile, and gasped. It was *Benazir Bhutto: An Intimate Portrait*—one of the titles that Ghostwriter had found!

Excited, Hector rifled through the box of biographies and history books. Then a noise startled him and he froze.

He relaxed when he realized it was just his mother and her friend, Leticia, clomping down the rickety stairs. With them was one of the women from the community garden, Barbara.

"What did you find, Hector?" his mother asked, noticing the box.

Hector quickly tucked the flaps over the books. "Just some books."

His mother came over and took a quick look. "They're not ours—they must belong to Roberto."

Hector nodded.

"Leticia is here to check the wiring and the plumbing," Maritza went on. "Barbara's going to help figure out where that water came from."

Or blood, Hector wanted to say.

Hector went back to his work table as his mother led the two women over to the circuit box.

"It was the strangest thing," he heard her say. "The lights went out, just like that. And we haven't had a single problem since."

Leticia peered inside the box and tested the switches, one at a time. "Everything looks fine," she said, shrugging.

"Good!" Maritza said, smiling. "Maybe the house was just getting used to us, the way we're getting used to it!"

"Maybe." Leticia winked at Hector and he smiled back.

"Come on upstairs," Maritza told the women. "I'll show you where we spotted the leak."

"See you later, Hector," Barbara called. "Good luck with your bench."

"Thanks," Hector replied.

As Maritza passed the back door, out of Hector's sight, she reached down and picked a tiny object off the floor.

After his mother and her friends had gone, Hector reached for his tools again. Suddenly all he wanted to do was forget about the case. He was tired of worrying about a ghost haunting his house. He began measuring the strips of wood. Soon he wasn't thinking about anything but making the bench.

But then an odd creaking sound broke through his concentration. The sound seemed to echo through the whole house.

Hector's head shot up. "It's the pipes," he told himself. His mother and her friends must be running water upstairs to check the plumbing.

But then another sound started, and Hector knew it wasn't the pipes. This sound was like a moan. It started softly, then grew louder and louder.

Whoooooooooooooo.

Hector's heart pounded. "Mom?" he said, his voice cracking. His eyes darted around the room. "Is that you?"

A voice replied, but it wasn't his mother's.

"This is my house," the eerie voice moaned. *"Get out of my house now!"*

CHAPTER 11

Hector flew up the basement stairs and flung open the door.

"Mom!" he shouted. The living room was empty.

Hector called out for his mother again.

This time she heard him. "I'm up here. We're fixing the bathroom," she yelled from the top floor.

Hector bolted up the steps and raced for the bathroom.

"Hector!" his mother said as he stood in the doorway, panting hard. "What happened?"

"You're not . . ." Hector gulped in air, then managed to choke out the rest of his words, "going to believe this."

"Believe what?" Leticia asked, looking at him with concern.

"I heard somebody. Down in the basement. It must be that ghost!"

"Ghost?" Maritza smiled. "What are you talking about?"

"The house is haunted, Mom!" Hector blurted out. "I should have told you sooner, but . . ." Hector poured out the whole story. He told his mother about the note. He told her about the stories X and Miles had told him, including the one about the man who had been murdered in this house on September 19, 1982. "X and Miles say it happened in my room, and the man's ghost still haunts the house!"

"Boy, Hector, you *are* new to the neighborhood!" Barbara exclaimed as she burst out laughing. "X and Miles are nice kids, but they are major practical jokers." She shook her head, still smiling. "This ghost is certainly one of their more elaborate creations."

Hector stared at her. "You never heard anything about the man who was murdered here?"

Barbara shook her head. "I've lived in this neighborhood for nearly eighteen years. I know for a fact that nobody was ever murdered in your house."

"What about those bloodstains?" Hector demanded. "And that moaning I heard downstairs?"

"The 'bloodstains' are just rusty water, Hector," Maritza said gently.

"That's right," Barbara said. "Your mom bought an old house. You've been hearing the pipes creak while we ran the water," she said matter-of-factly.

Hector shook his head. He kept silent. But he was positive he'd heard something else—a terrible, eerie voice saying, *"This is my house. Get out of my house now!"*

His mother put an arm around him.

"Our house isn't haunted, honey," she said. "I know the basement is kind of spooky, but Leticia is going to help me put some more lights down there. And I'm going to talk to those neighborhood boys," she went on. "I want these ridiculous stories about our house to stop right now."

"No!" Hector started panicking. The last thing he wanted was for his mother to say anything to X and Miles. "Please don't do that, Mom. It'll make everything worse."

"I think he's right, Maritza," Barbara said. "Knowing X and Miles, they'll just give Hector a harder time if you say something. If Hector ignores them, they'll get bored and switch back to annoying Marion."

"Okay." Maritza nodded slowly. Then she peered into Hector's face. "Are you sure you're okay, honey?"

"I'm fine," Hector lied.

"Good," his mother said, satisfied. "I love this house, and this neighborhood, and I want you to be happy here, too." Suddenly she remembered something. She reached into her pocket and pulled out a small object. "I found this in the basement, near the back door. It isn't yours—is it?"

Hector took the object from his mother. It was a small, metal badge with a pin attached to the back. As Hector flipped it over, he drew in a sharp breath.

Stamped all over the front were the letters *BSM* . . . *BSM* . . . *BSM.*

CHAPTER 12

On Saturday morning, the team rode the subway back to 138 Sullivan Avenue. On the way Hector told his friends about the ghost's visit to the basement.

"Are you sure you heard a *ghost* moaning?" Tina said. "Maybe it was the wind, or the pipes creaking, like your mom's friend said."

"I'm positive," Hector insisted. "Maybe the pipes were creaking, too, but I know I heard a ghost's voice."

"So Hector . . ." Jamal leaned closer. "What does a ghost sound like?"

"*Whoooooooooo . . .*" Hector started to imitate the eerie moaning.

Jamal's lip quivered and then he burst out

laughing. "Gotcha," he declared as he and Alex high-fived.

"Very funny," Hector retorted. He was angry. It was one thing that his mother didn't believe him about the ghost, but he expected the team to take him seriously. "Fine, don't believe me," he said. "I'm just telling you what I heard, okay?"

There was an uncomfortable silence for the next few minutes. When the team members stood up to exit at their stop, Jamal looked apologetic. "Sorry, Hector," he said. "I didn't mean to make fun of you. I know something's going on at your house. I'm just not sure it's a real ghost."

"It's okay," Hector replied. "But don't expect me to laugh about all this yet—even if it is a joke." He swallowed hard. "This house is my mother's dream, Jamal. It means a lot to her, and if it's haunted . . ."

Jamal nodded solemnly. "We'll find the ghost, buddy. I promise."

As Hector and Jamal followed the others out onto the street, Gaby turned to Hector. "Did you get Roberto's phone number from your mom?"

"No," Hector admitted. "I couldn't figure out a way to ask her for his number without telling her why I needed it." He reached into his pocket and pulled out a slip of paper. "But I did find his last name on some of her papers. Maybe we can look him up in the phone book. His last name is . . ." Hector read the name he'd jotted down. "Garcia."

"*Garcia*?" Alex echoed. "Are you sure?"

"Yes," Hector insisted. "Garcia." As he said the name again, he realized it wasn't the first time he'd heard it.

● Attention, Reader: Do you remember where the team saw the name "R. Garcia"?

—Ghostwriter

Hector stopped short on the sidewalk. "Oh, my gosh," he said. "Garcia was the name on the mailbox at one-thirty-eight Sullivan Avenue!"

The whole team was looking at him.

"I don't get it," Casey said.

"I don't really get it, either," Hector said excitedly. "But it must mean something. The guy who lives at one-thirty-eight Sullivan is Roberto Garcia—the man who used to live in my house!"

Hector felt Jamal's hand on his shoulder. "Maybe we're finally about to meet your ghost, Hector."

* * *

"Mr. Garcia?" Lenni said as a tall, skinny man with a dark mustache came to the door at 138 Sullivan Avenue.

"Yes," the man replied, nodding. Hector guessed he was in his mid-sixties. "That's me."

Jamal started to explain that they had come to ask him some questions about his old house. But as soon as Jamal mentioned 101 Ellington Street, the color drained from Mr. Garcia's face.

"Is one of you Hector Carrero?" he asked.

Hector nodded, surprised. "I'm Hector," he started, "but how did you—"

"Oh, no." Mr. Garcia interrupted him. "The ghost has visited you and your mother, too!"

The team members exchanged glances as Mr. Garcia held open the door. "Please come in," he murmured.

Hector's palms were sweaty as he sat down next to Gaby on the couch inside Mr. Garcia's living room. While Mr. Garcia got himself a glass of water, Hector glanced nervously around the house. The living room was small and comfortable, with several old chairs and two tall bookcases crammed with books, mostly about history.

Mr. Garcia was still pale and his hands were trembling as he carried the glass of water into the living room. "Where do I begin?" he mumbled.

"What made you think that a ghost had visited Hector and his mother?" Tina prodded him.

"Did you see any sign of a ghost when you were living there?" Casey chimed in.

"Yes." Mr. Garcia sighed deeply as he sat down. "I bought that house six years ago from Marion Wolf," he explained. "It was shortly after her husband died. And at first, everything was fine. But then . . ." Mr. Garcia shook his head and looked pained. "About six months after I moved in, strange things started to happen."

"Like what?" Hector asked.

"I'd come home from work and find my things had been moved around."

"Was anything ever missing?" Alex asked.

"No." Mr. Garcia shook his head. "It was like somebody was just wandering around inside the house, looking things over. I changed the lock on the front door, but it didn't help. I still had the sense that someone was there in the house with me. Sometimes at night I'd even see strange lights flickering in my room. And then . . ." His words trailed off for a second. "That terrible moaning started."

"Moaning?" Hector shot a look at his friends. "Did the ghost ever say anything to you?" he asked.

Mr. Garcia reached for his glass and gulped down some more water. "Yes," he said. "Over and over it would say, 'This is *my* house. Get out of my house!' I had the terrible feeling that . . ."

"What?" Gaby sat on the edge of her seat.

Mr. Garcia avoided Hector's eyes. "I thought something terrible would happen if I stayed," he finished.

There was a long silence. Hector could feel his heart thumping in his chest.

Jamal looked as cool as ever. "Did you ever ask Marion Wolf if anything like this had happened when she was living there?" he asked.

"No," Mr. Garcia said softly. "Her husband had passed away. She didn't want to sell her house and leave behind all those memories, but she had no choice. I thought my stories about a ghost would only upset her."

"So why did you sell the house?" Alex asked.

"As I said, things kept getting more frightening," Mr. Garcia told him. "I started looking around for an apartment. I wasn't sure I was really going to move out until . . ." This time he looked at Hector. "I saw the ghost with my own eyes."

Hector stiffened. "You *saw* the ghost?"

Mr. Garcia seemed far away. "One night, about

two years ago, I'd gone to bed early. I was sound asleep when that terrible moaning started. 'Get out! Get out of my house,' the ghost was saying. When I woke up and looked around . . ." Mr. Garcia closed his eyes. "I saw a shimmering, white shape in the middle of my room. It had long, bony fingers, and the most hideous, empty-looking eyes. . . ."

Mr. Garcia opened his eyes and looked at Alex. "That's what made me sell the house. That—and the feeling that something dreadful would happen if I didn't leave."

Alex nodded, satisfied. But Hector felt anger boiling up inside him. He shot to his feet. "How could you do that?" he shouted at Mr. Garcia. "How could you sell a haunted house to my mother!"

"It was wrong, Hector," Mr. Garcia said softly. "I had regrets after she bought it. That's why I left the warning."

"What warning?" Hector snapped. "You never warned us."

"Yes, I did." Mr. Garcia stared at him. "Didn't you find the note?"

"The note?" Alex exclaimed. "That was from you?"

"Yes." Mr. Garcia nodded. "Leaving that note behind was the only thing I could think of to do."

"*Hmpf.*" Hector folded his arms and turned away. *Big deal,* he thought. So Mr. Garcia had left a note. That didn't even come close to making up for the fact that he'd sold Hector's mother a haunted house.

"Do you know those boys, X and Miles, who live in your old neighborhood?" Lenni was asking.

"Everyone knows those two," Mr. Garcia said with a trace of a smile. "Their favorite pastime is trying to drive poor Marion Wolf crazy!"

"Did they ever tell you any stories about a guy being murdered at one-oh-one on September 19, 1982?" Jamal asked.

"No!" Mr. Garcia looked at Jamal with a startled expression. "Is that true?"

"We don't think so," Jamal replied cautiously.

"Our guess is that X and Miles made up the story to spook Hector," Lenni chimed in.

"Knowing them, that's entirely possible," Mr. Garcia said. "But how do you explain the other things? Like the ghost visiting my room? And the moaning at all hours of the day and night?"

"We can't explain those things," Alex admitted. "But we're working on it."

Jamal stood up. "Thank you for your time, Mr. Garcia."

He nodded, staring thoughtfully at Hector. "It's the least I can do," he said. As he walked the team to the door, he touched Hector's arm. "You and your mom haven't come across a box of books, have you?"

Hector looked at him and nodded.

"Oh, good." Mr. Garcia looked relieved. "I moved out so quickly, I left some things behind."

"Do you want that dresser in my room back, too?" Hector asked.

"That actually belonged to Marion's husband," Mr. Garcia replied. "She left it behind when she moved next door. You and your mom can keep that. I'll be on Ellington Street later, having dinner with friends. Could I stop by then to pick up the box?"

"I guess so," Hector said coldly. He was still angry. Without saying good-bye, Hector turned around and stalked off to join his friends. He'd give Mr. Garcia the books, he decided, but after that, Hector never wanted to see him again.

As the team rode home on the train, they talked about what Mr. Garcia had told them.

"His stories are so hard to believe," Gaby said.

"Come on, a ghost visited his room at night and told him to leave the house?" She shook her head. "I don't think so."

"But that's what Hector said happened in the basement!" Casey protested. "Maybe Mr. Garcia *is* telling the truth."

"I've been thinking," Tina said. She looked at Hector. "Mr. Garcia's the one who left you the note. Maybe he's the one who's been trying to scare you, too."

"But why, Tina?" Jamal asked, running a hand through his hair. "Why would he want to scare Hector and his mom?"

"I don't know," she admitted.

"Let's at least add him to the Suspects list," Alex suggested.

Hector handed him the casebook.

"I still think that X and Miles are involved in all this," Lenni said. "Maybe they managed to trick Mr. Garcia into thinking that there was a ghost."

Hector had been listening quietly while his friends talked about the case. Suddenly he couldn't keep his feelings in anymore.

"Maybe the ghost is really a ghost, you guys!" he burst out. "Like Casey said, maybe Roberto is telling the truth, just like I'm telling the truth!"

"We're not saying you're lying, Hector," Alex

said calmly. "We're just trying to come up with an explanation for the things you've seen and heard."

Hector nodded, then bit his lip to keep from saying more. But as he listened to his friends start up the conversation again, he wanted to scream. Casey was the only one who seemed to believe that the ghost might be real.

Despite his anger at Mr. Garcia, Hector believed his stories about moans in the middle of the night and eerie lights shining in his bedroom. Hector had seen Mr. Garcia's fingers tremble and his face go pale when he talked about the ghost.

Whoever—or whatever—was haunting Hector's house had frightened Mr. Garcia away for good.

CHAPTER 13

When the team got to Hector's house, Marion
Wolf was coming out of her house next door.

"How are you, Mrs. Wolf?" Gaby asked.

"Terrible," Marion groaned. "My lower back is
killing me, and I haven't even gotten to work yet.
Not to mention the fact that I'll be on my feet all
night long."

"Sounds tough," Alex said.

"You got that right, cookie," she went on. "You
know something, there was a time when I didn't
have to work, and . . ." Marion stopped talking.
For a second her eyes fixed on Hector's house.
"Well, never mind that," she said abruptly.
"There's no use thinking about how things could
have been." She let out a sigh. "Tell your mother

I'll bring her some sticky buns in the morning, Hector," she added as she headed for the subway.

"Having her for a neighbor can't be all bad," Jamal said as Hector pushed open the door to his house. "She brings you stuff from the bakery."

"I guess," Hector grumbled. "At least sticky buns sound better than those prune pastry things she brought over yesterday."

Everybody laughed. Except Alex.

He stood stone-still in the entrance hall. "I just thought of something," he said slowly. "Maybe it's Marion."

"Huh?" Lenni said.

"Maybe what's Marion?" Hector asked.

"The ghost!"

"I don't think so, Alex," Hector replied.

"Didn't you see the way Marion was looking at your house, Hector?" he said. "It was sort of—"

"Spooky," Gaby filled in. "She was staring at your house as if she really missed it or something, Hector."

"So?" Hector couldn't believe that Alex and Gaby really thought Marion was the ghost. "Maybe she does miss the house. She lived here for twenty years."

"I'm telling you, Hector," Alex insisted. "The expression on her face was weird."

"Why don't we ask Ghostwriter to check her house for clues?" Jamal suggested.

Everybody looked to Hector.

"Sure. I guess so." He shrugged. But inwardly he was thinking it was a waste of time. Why would Marion want him to think the house was haunted?

Hector pulled out the casebook. The team sat around the kitchen table while he wrote a note to Ghostwriter.

"Ask him if he can find anything about *BSM*," Gaby said, looking at the list of evidence. "That's the one that keeps showing up."

"We need your help again, Ghostwriter," Hector wrote. "Can you look around Marion Wolf's house to see if you can find anything that says '*BSM*'?"

There was a sparkle of light as Ghostwriter read the team's message and the list of evidence. Then he took off.

By the time Hector had poured glasses of iced tea for everybody, Ghostwriter was back.

Hector watched the casebook as the first message appeared.

This week—BSM.

"Huh?" Jamal said. "What does that mean?"

Tina grabbed her pen. "Ghostwriter, we don't get it. Are there any other words nearby?" she wrote.

Ghostwriter disappeared, then returned a moment later.

Think before you bite, he wrote.

" 'Think before you bite?' " Lenni read the message aloud.

"That's from Marion's refrigerator," Hector said, smiling. "I think she's on a diet."

Next came three letters: *ORK.* They were followed by several other words:

        on. 2–5 P.M.
        ues. 4–9 P.M.
        at. 12–6 P.M.

Gaby peered at them closely. "The letters *ORK* must be part of the word *work*," she guessed.

"And those other words look like the days of the week," Tina said, "with the first letter missing."

"Hey, maybe it's Marion's work schedule," Lenni said.

"Maybe," Hector said. "But what does that have to do with *BSM,* you guys?" Hector said.

"Nothing so far," Jamal said, frowning at the clues. "Ghostwriter," he wrote, "can you find 'BSM' anywhere else in Marion's house?"

Hector tapped his foot impatiently while the team waited for Ghostwriter to return. Then he watched the letters in the casebook swirl into another message:

Property of BSM.

"Why does Marion have something that says 'Property of BSM' in her house?" Casey asked.

"I don't know, Casey," Alex replied. "But *BSM* must stand for something. We have to figure out what."

"Hey, Hector. Do you have a phone book?" Jamal asked.

Hector nodded and reached into the kitchen closet. Hector and Jamal looked up the letters, but they couldn't find anything under *BSM*.

"It's so frustrating," Gaby said. "I know I've seen those letters before. I just can't remember where."

"Me either," Hector murmured. But this time as he looked down at the open phone book it came to him. A sound rose in his throat.

Everyone looked at him.

"X's T-shirt!" Hector cried. "The day I met X and Miles, X had on a T-shirt that had the letters *BSM* printed all over it."

"Aha!" Lenni said.

His excitement mounting, Hector reached into his pocket and held out the metal badge with the letters BSM all over it that his mother had found in the basement. "Do you think this belongs to X?" Hector asked the team.

As soon as she saw the badge, Casey recognized it. "I know where that's from!" she said. "The Brooklyn Science Museum. They give out those buttons when you go inside. My class went on a trip there a few weeks ago."

"*B-S-M*!" Jamal spelled out. "Casey's right."

"But Ghostwriter found *BSM* in Marion's house," Alex reminded them. "Not on X's T-shirt."

"Ugh!" Tina groaned. "I feel like we're *never* going to figure this case out. One minute I think Mr. Garcia has something to do with the ghost; the next minute I'm convinced it's Marion, or X and Miles."

"I have an idea," Casey spoke up. "Why don't we go to the museum and look around. We might find out something. Even if we don't, you guys will love how cool it is."

"What's so cool about it?" Alex asked.

"All the exhibits are designed for kids," Casey explained. "The people who work there dress up in weird glasses and lab coats, and pretend to be mad scientists. And they have a great computer room."

"Mad scientists?" Alex repeated. "That does sound fun."

Hector glanced at the clock. It was after three. "It's too late to go today," he said, disappointed. "I promised my mom I'd help her strip the wallpaper in the dining room this afternoon."

Jamal nodded. "Okay. Why don't we head over to the museum first thing tomorrow morning?"

After his friends had left, Hector went into the dining room, where his mother had already started scraping the old red-flowered wallpaper off the walls.

Hector wrinkled his nose. "Boy, is this stuff ugly."

"I'll say," his mother agreed. Then she smiled. "Although that's not what Marion said when she came over yesterday with the prune pastries. . . ." Hector laughed as his mother put a hand on her hip and did an almost perfect imitation of Marion saying how lovely the room looked—just as it was.

"I think Marion wants the whole house to stay

exactly the same way forever," Hector said, smiling.

His mother nodded. "She lived here for so many years. I guess she still thinks of this as her home."

Hector flopped down on one of the dining-room chairs. He remembered the sad expression on Marion's face an hour before, when she'd been looking at the house. "How did her husband die exactly, Mom?" he asked.

"He had a heart attack," Maritza said. "Marion told me he wasn't sick a day in his life, and then one day, coming home from work . . ." She snapped her fingers. "He went, just like that. It happened over six years ago, but I think Marion is still mourning him. They were married almost twenty-five years."

Hector stood up and started helping his mother scrape the walls.

"Look at this, Hector!" Maritza called a few minutes later as she peeled off the next strip of the red-flowered paper. "Someone drew all over the wall before it was papered!"

Hector went over to where his mother was working and looked for himself. Sure enough, the white wall underneath the paper was covered with drawings. The pictures of a house and a playground looked as if they'd been drawn by a child, but the other drawings, Hector noticed, were probably drawn by an adult—a talented adult.

He smiled at a cartoon of a strongman flexing his enormous muscles. Next to it was another funny picture of a hippopotamus floating on its back in a pond. "These are great!" he exclaimed.

As Hector looked more closely at the drawing of the hippo, he noticed a signature scrawled below the drawing. "Look, Mom. It's signed by Herman Wolf."

"That's Marion's husband," Maritza said, taking a closer look. "And see this, Hector . . ." She pointed to a horizontal line near the hippo. "This must be an old chart for Marion's son, Brent, when he was only about six years old. Forty-six inches," she read out loud. She gave Hector a wistful look. "I remember when you were that small."

"Don't get mushy on me, Mom," Hector warned her, smiling.

For the next few minutes, Hector and his mother stood together, looking at the pictures.

"Brent and his dad must have drawn these pictures fifteen years ago," Maritza mused. "So many things have changed since then."

Hector nodded his agreement. Fifteen years ago,

the Wolfs were still living here and Herman was still alive.

His mother suddenly put an arm around Hector. "Don't grow up too fast—okay?"

"I thought you were glad that I'm getting bigger, Mom," Hector joked. "Now I can help you with all the chores."

To his surprise, his mother didn't laugh. She just shook her head. "Time goes by too quickly," she said sadly. "And sometimes I'm just not ready for you to stop being my little boy."

Hector let his mother hug him before they both went back to work.

After dinner, Hector remembered the box of books for Mr. Garcia. He ran down to the basement, grabbed the carton, then shot back up the stairs. He hadn't been in the basement since the day when he'd heard the moaning, and he was definitely not going to stay any longer than he had to.

Hector was about to place the books near the front door when something caught his eye. A book poking out from the middle of the pile had a big, bold letter *X* on the cover.

"Whoa . . ." Hector murmured. He reached into the box for the book. It was an old paperback.

The title, *The Autobiography of Malcolm X,* was printed in bold type across the front.

Hector's heart skipped a beat. Could this be the *X* that Ghostwriter had found the other day?

Hector left the box by the front door and went into the dining room to tell his mother that Mr. Garcia would be coming over later. Luckily she was so busy picking up the scraps of wallpaper and stuffing them into garbage bags, she didn't think to ask Hector when he'd talked to Mr. Garcia.

Instead she handed him an empty trash bag. "Will you please collect the trash from upstairs, honey?"

"Sure."

Hector took the big plastic bag and headed upstairs.

In his room, he emptied the small garbage pail near his bed. As the trash tumbled into the plastic bag, Hector spotted the old newspaper he'd found in the dresser that Mr. Garcia had left behind.

As before, the paper was folded open to the real estate section. But this time Hector noticed that three addresses had been circled in bright-red ink:

12 Lincoln Street
138 Sullivan Avenue
413 Third Street

These were the addresses that Ghostwriter had found, Hector realized. This paper was probably left over from Mr. Garcia's search for a new apartment.

Hector wondered if he'd find the other clue Ghostwriter had found—the date September 19, 1982—somewhere nearby.

Impulsively, Hector dumped the entire contents of the trash bag onto the floor and started sifting through the crumpled papers.

As Hector set aside the neatly folded, white handkerchief he had found in the dresser, he spotted something else. Written in spidery handwriting on the back of an old photo was the date *September 19, 1982*.

Hector's heart pounded as he turned the picture over. He hadn't noticed it the other day, but this picture had been taken in front of his own house. Standing in front of the narrow, brick house at 101 Ellington Street was a younger, slimmer Marion. Her mouth was open in a wide grin, and Hector saw that her hair had been longer back then, and blond. Next to her on the right was little Brent, a wide gap in his smile from two missing front teeth. Hector knew instantly who the tall man on Marion's left must be—her husband, Herman Wolf.

Curious, Hector stared at the Wolf he'd never

met. Herman had been as thin as he was tall, with a long, pale face and dark, intense eyes.

As Hector stared at Herman's eyes, the blood in his veins turned ice-cold.

"Oh, my gosh," Hector gasped. He'd remembered something that Marion had told him the day they'd first met.

His eyes went back to the photo. Suddenly it all fell into place. Hector had found the ghost who'd been haunting his house for the last six years.

CHAPTER 14

Hector had to get in touch with the team right away. *Wait until they hear this,* he thought. While he was staring at the picture of the Wolfs, Hector had remembered Marion telling him that her son worked at the BSM.

Hector found a sheet of plain white paper in his backpack and wrote RALLY H in big, black letters.

Green lights danced over the letters as Ghostwriter carried the message to Jamal, Casey, Gaby, Alex, Tina, and Lenni.

"Please hurry, Ghostwriter," Hector whispered. He paced the floor as he waited for the rest of the team to meet him at his house.

* * *

When Gaby, Alex, and Tina arrived a short while later, rain was coming down hard and the wind was whipping through the trees in front of Hector's house.

"Hi, Hector." Gaby handed him her wet coat. "Guess who we bumped into!"

"Marion?" Hector said anxiously.

"No." Alex shook his head. "Mr. Garcia. We saw him going into the house across the street."

"He said he was having dinner with a friend," Hector reminded them.

Tina raised her eyebrows. "That's what he *said*. . . ." she muttered.

Hector led them up to his room, where the rest of the team was waiting.

"So what's up with the case, Hector?" Jamal asked. "Casey and I had a hard time explaining to my mom why we had to go out in the pouring rain."

Hector told them that he had remembered that Brent worked at the BSM.

"That's right," Jamal said, tapping himself on the side of his head. "I forgot about that."

Gaby looked back and forth between Jamal and Hector. "So? What does that have to do with anything, you guys?"

"I'm still figuring it out, Gaby," Hector said. "But I think . . ." He hurried over to the mahogany dresser. "I think I know who the ghost is now," he said, holding up the old picture of the Wolfs.

The team stared at the snapshot.

"See this man?" Hector pointed to Herman Wolf. "This is Marion's dead husband."

"Hector," Alex said in a warning tone. "Don't tell me you think that Marion's husband is haunting—"

Before Alex could finish, a loud clap of thunder boomed outside.

Casey jumped and so did Hector.

Through the window, Hector saw a bolt of lightning tear through the dark sky. A second later the lights went out.

Everyone groaned.

"I can't believe the power's out," Alex said.

Thunder rumbled again, rattling the windows of the house.

"You guys okay up there?" Hector's mother yelled from downstairs.

"We're fine, Mom."

"I'm on my way up," she replied.

A minute later Maritza knocked and entered

Hector's room. She was holding a lit candle and had a flashlight tucked under her arm.

"Here you go," she said, handing Hector the flashlight. "I'll be right back. I'm going downstairs to check the circuit box."

"The circuit box?" Jamal echoed. "Didn't the *storm* knock out the power, Ms. Carrero?"

Even in the dim candlelight, Hector could see the worried look in his mother's eyes.

"I thought it was the storm, too," she said, "until I noticed that everybody else on the block still has power."

Hector glanced out the window. Sure enough, the streetlamps along Ellington Street were on, and he could see lights in the house across the street. When he looked out the other window, he saw lights on at the Wolfs' house, too.

The room was silent as Maritza turned around and went back downstairs.

Then Casey echoed Hector's thought. "This is so spooky," she murmured. "Why didn't the power go out in the rest of the neighborhood?"

Lenni looked at Gaby. "Did I hear you telling Hector that you saw Mr. Garcia on the block?"

Gaby nodded.

Alarmed, Jamal looked at Hector. "What about

that picture of Herman Wolf, Hector? What were you just about to tell us?"

Hector opened his mouth to reply. But before any words came out, he saw a shimmering white light dancing in his room.

Whooooooo.

Then a terrible moan filled the air.

Alex gasped, his voice filled with panic. "What's that?" he demanded. "What's that thing in the middle of the room?"

No one said a word in reply.

Hector stared at the huge, white shape taking form in the center of the room. The ghost's eyes were gaping holes, as if they'd been gouged from its head, and its outstretched fingers were long and quivering.

"Get out . . ." the ghost moaned. Hector could hear the ghost breathe, as if it were gasping for air. "This is my house. . . ." Then the ghost pointed a long, thin finger at Hector. "You do not belong. . . ."

Hector couldn't hear the rest of what the ghost said as Tina's horrified scream ripped through the air.

CHAPTER 15

Hector was still staring at the hideous figure when the room was suddenly flooded with bright light.

The power was back on. For a moment, everyone was blinded. When they could see clearly again, the ghost was gone.

The team members stood frozen, horrified expressions on their faces.

"Oh, my gosh! Oh, my gosh!" Gaby was saying over and over. "I can't believe it. A real ghost. I saw a real ghost."

Just then Maritza burst through the door. "What's the matter?" she demanded. "Who was screaming?"

"We saw the ghost!" Casey blurted out.

"What?" Maritza exclaimed.

Casey told her what they had seen.

"Hector," Maritza started, giving him a warning look. "Are you trying to scare your friends with those crazy stories that X and Miles told you?"

"No, Mom," Hector insisted. "We really saw something." He was about to say more, but he decided his mother had enough to worry about with the electricity going out. "Maybe it was just lights outside or something," he said. Then he quickly changed the subject. "Did you check the circuit box again, Mom?"

"Yes," Maritza said with a frown. "For some reason, the switch tripped again. "I'm going to call Leticia right now and tell her." She looked at Hector. "Are you sure you guys are okay?"

"We're fine," he assured her. "Go ahead."

But as soon as Maritza left the room, Lenni turned to Hector. "I am totally spooked," she said in a trembling voice. "I was convinced that X and Miles were tricking you, Hector, and now . . ."

Tina looked pale and shaken, too. "That ghost was the scariest thing I've ever seen," she said. She took a deep breath to calm herself. "I'm sorry I didn't take you more seriously, Hector. I thought you were overreacting because of the new house."

Hector hardly heard them. He had crept over to

the window, and his eyes were riveted on something next door.

Jamal was watching his friend. "What's up, Hector?" he whispered softly.

Hector held a finger to his lips as he beckoned for Jamal to shut off the light again. Then he waved his friends over to see what he'd been watching across the way. The shade was up in the window of the bedroom at Marion's house, and a large white figure was moving about inside the room.

"Oh, my gosh," Gaby gasped. "It's the ghost again!"

CHAPTER 16

Outside the rain had slowed to a drizzle. Puddles dotted the street, and a smoky fog drifted up toward the streetlamps.

The knot in Hector's stomach tightened as he walked slowly up the path in front of Marion's house. His friends were close behind.

We're about to do it, he thought. *We're about to come face to face with the ghost.*

The team stood for a moment on the Wolfs' stoop in silence. Hector reached into his pocket, where he could feel the tiny badge from the BSM.

Alex nodded at Hector. "Go ahead, buddy," he said softly.

"Okay." Hector took a deep breath. With trembling fingers, he banged the brass knocker hard against the door. Behind him, he felt Gaby gripping the back of his shirt, and he heard Alex clearing his throat loudly.

At first no one answered Hector's knock.

He was reaching for the knocker again when he heard slow, shuffling steps approaching. Then, as the heavy door swung open, Hector instinctively backed away.

A tall figure in white loomed in the doorway, bathed in an eerie glow from the yellow porch light.

Hector swallowed hard as he stared at the ghost. "Yeah?" It was Brent Wolf's voice. He was wearing the white lab coat from his job at the Brooklyn Science Museum. "What do you want?"

Casey's eyes were open wide. "Oh, my gosh," she murmured. "Hector, you were right!"

"Right about what?" Brent demanded.

"About you, Brent. You've been trying to make Hector think his new house was haunted," Jamal said.

"What?" Brent laughed loudly. "You've been reading too many horror books, Hector."

Hector felt a flare of anger. "No I haven't, Brent," he retorted. "I still haven't figured out everything, but I know that you've been playing tricks on me and my mother."

"That's crazy," Brent scoffed.

"It *sounds* crazy," Hector said. "But I have proof." He opened his hand and showed Brent the BSM badge. "I found this in our basement after the first time you turned off our electricity. You still have a key to the door down there, right?"

"Get real, Hector," Brent said. "I have more important things to do than sneak around your basement, trying to spook a bunch of kids."

"Oh, yeah?" Before he had time to think about what he was doing, Hector shot past Brent into the house.

"Hey!" Brent shouted. "Where do you think you're going?"

Hector tore up the stairs. Brent took off after him, and the rest of the team followed.

Upstairs, Hector looked around quickly. The layout of Marion's house was just like the layout of his. Brent's room had to be off to the left.

As soon as Hector burst into Brent's room, he found all the proof he needed. A long table had been placed under the window that looked out on the alleyway and Hector's house. On top of the table was a laser machine, a mirror, and several lenses. Hector also spotted several small bottles—

chemicals for developing film—and an expensive-looking CD player.

Brent ran into the room behind Hector. "If you don't get out of here right now," he warned in a threatening voice, "I'm going to—"

"Look at this!" Hector shouted to the rest of the team behind Brent. "Brent's been shooting holograms through the window!"

"What?" Casey said. She turned to Jamal. "What's a hologram?" she asked.

"A three-dimensional image that's made with photographic equipment," Jamal explained. "I think Hector's saying Brent projected a hologram into Hector's room. That's why the ghost looked so real."

Jamal looked at the supplies on Brent's table more closely. The laser and two of the lenses were labeled, PROPERTY OF BSM.

"You must have learned how to shoot holograms at the science museum," he said to Brent.

Brent didn't say anything. But as he sank down on his bed, his tall frame seemed to crumple.

"I still don't get it," Alex said. "Why did you do it?" he asked Brent.

Brent just shook his head.

"I think I know," Hector said softly. He reached into his pocket again. This time he pulled out the old, black-and-white photo of the Wolf family and handed it to Brent. "This is why you did it, right, Brent?" he said.

Slowly Brent took the photo. Hector saw him swallow hard as he looked at it. "My dad used to keep this in his dresser drawer," Brent said in a choked voice. "This is my mom and me and my dad in front of our old . . ."

"House," Hector finished for him.

Brent nodded as he looked at Hector. "I didn't want to move," he said. "My father and I were really close, and when he died . . . I know it sounds stupid," he went on, "but I felt like if we could just stay in the house, then somehow my dad wouldn't really be gone."

Hector noticed Lenni and Tina exchanging sympathetic looks. In spite of everything that Brent had done, it was hard not to feel sorry for him.

"But my mom said we had to move," Brent went on. "Without my dad's income, we couldn't afford to own a house. She kept telling me we were only going next door, but it didn't matter. To me, it wasn't home."

"What made you think of haunting Mr. Garcia's house?" Jamal asked.

"I got the idea after he bought the house from my mother," Brent said, sounding sheepish. "At first I just used to sneak into the house to look around, but then I got the idea to spook him. I thought if I made him think the house was haunted, he'd sell it back to my mother for a really low price." He shrugged. "Once I got the job at the museum and learned about making holograms, it was easy to convince him that the house was haunted."

"And then we came along," Hector said, "and you did it all again."

Brent nodded. "The problem was, when Mr. Garcia put the house on the market, my mom didn't want to buy it back. She said it was still too expensive and too much work for her to keep up on her own. I thought I could convince her to buy it the next time it was for sale."

"Until I saw that ghost tonight, I thought X and Miles were trying to play a joke on Hector," Lenni said. "Did they know what you were up to?"

"Not exactly," Brent said. "They had heard some of Mr. Garcia's stories and thought he just imagined everything. Then when Hector moved in, I suggested that we play a little joke on him and exaggerate the stories." A small smile crossed his face. "Naturally X and Miles thought spooking Hector would be lots of fun."

"It worked," Hector remarked. "That wild story

about the guy being murdered upstairs in my bedroom . . ." He shook his head. "Now *that* spooked me!"

While the team asked Brent more questions, Hector sat quietly at the desk in Brent's room. He'd figured most of Brent's scheme out beforehand. But there was one thing he hadn't really understood until tonight, when he'd seen Brent's face. He hadn't realized how lonely and desperate Brent had been since his father's death.

The sound of the front door being unlocked startled Hector from his thoughts.

"Brent!" a familiar voice boomed up the stairs. "Did you make this mess in the living room?"

Brent groaned. "Guess who's home . . ." he murmured.

"How many times do I have to tell you?" Marion went on. "I'm not Superwoman. I can't keep putting in these long hours at the bakery and then come home to a house that looks like a pigsty. If you think . . ."

Brent rolled his eyes as Marion continued to rant from the bottom floor. "Sometimes my mother can really drive me crazy," he said.

"I know exactly what you mean," said Hector, and they both grinned.

A moment later Jamal stood up. "It's late. If Casey and I don't get home soon, my mother's going to think *we've* turned into ghosts."

"So long, Brent," Alex said.

Hector's friends started down the stairs, but he stayed behind in Brent's room for a moment. "I wanted to tell you something," he started. He felt embarrassed but he made himself continue. "I think I understand how you felt about leaving your house."

Brent looked at him, surprised.

"I was excited about our new house at first," Hector explained. "But now . . . I miss our old apartment," he admitted. "It was small, but my mom and I lived there for a long time. I keep thinking about it and wishing we still lived there."

"You'll get used to the new place soon," Brent said.

"Yeah . . . I guess so." Hector stood up, a small smile on his lips. "Maybe it'll be a little easier now that the ghost is gone."

Brent smiled and started to hand back the black-and-white photo, but Hector shook his head. "Keep it," he told Brent. "I know it's not the same as giving you back your house, but I bet your dad would want you to have it."

"Thanks, Hector," Brent said. "I'm really sorry I scared you," he went on. "I'm going to return the hologram stuff to the museum, you know. I'm done haunting houses."

"Good," Hector replied. He was halfway to the door when he stopped for the second time. "You look a lot like your dad, you know," he added softly. Brent smiled.

The team was waiting for Hector outside in the rain.

"Good job, Hector," Jamal said as Hector came out. "That was really cool how you figured out what Brent was up to."

"I'll say," Gaby agreed. "This case had me totally stumped. In fact . . ." She wrinkled her nose. "There's one clue I still can't figure out. . . . Remember that big *X* Ghostwriter found in your house? Where was that from?"

"Yeah." Lenni nodded. "That's what made me think that X and Miles were the ghost."

Hector told his friends about how he'd found the book, *The Autobiography of Malcolm X,* in Mr. Garcia's box.

As the team walked toward Hector's house, he felt relief wash over him. "For the first time since we moved in, I won't have to worry about bumping into a ghost in the middle of the night!" he said.

"Now you can concentrate on unpacking," Lenni said, teasing him.

"You sound just like my mother!" Hector complained. But he was smiling.

"Hey, look who's here," Casey said suddenly.

Hector looked in the distance where Casey was pointing. Near the billboard for the Brooklyn Science Museum there was a swirl of green light.

"Ghostwriter!" Hector said.

The team watched as Ghostwriter rearranged the letters on the billboard.

Bummer! I was hoping to meet another ghost.

Jamal chuckled. "Ghostwriter sounds pretty disappointed that the ghost was a fake."

"Maybe next time we'll find a *real* . . ." Hector started to say. But then something struck him. In a way, the team *had* encountered a real ghost. Brent Wolf was the one who'd been doing all the spooky things. But his father, Herman Wolf, was the one who'd been haunting Hector's house. Six years ago, Herman had died, but his presence had lingered at 101 Ellington Street. . . .

Until tonight, Hector thought. Maybe after tonight, Herman Wolf's presence would finally be gone from Hector's house.

Just then the light outside Hector's house flipped on, and the front door opened. "Hector?" his mother called. "Are you out there?"

Gaby nudged him. "Your mother sounds worried, Hector. You'd better go in."

Hector nodded. But first he had something to say to his friends. "You guys are the best," he said. "Thanks."

Alex grinned. "I'm glad the team finally busted your ghost, Hector."

"Who else ya gonna call when there's a ghost in the 'hood?" Jamal chimed in.

CHAPTER 17

Hector was in his room a few weeks later when he heard a loud knock on the front door.

"Anybody home?" a familiar voice called.

"Hi, Ruben!" Maritza said. She let her brother into the house, then yelled up the stairs to Hector. "Uncle Ruben's here, honey. It's time to go to the barbecue."

"I'm coming, Mom," Hector called back. He quickly pulled a T-shirt on over his shorts, then scanned his room for his Yankees cap. He wasn't going anywhere until he found it.

Hector had spent the last few weeks unpacking his things and settling into his new room. Now baseball posters covered almost every inch of the white walls, and his autographed Roberto Clemente baseball card was proudly displayed on his dresser—the same dresser that had once belonged to Herman Wolf. Hector figured it was just about the only sign left of the ghost.

The walls in the kitchen were still pea green. . . . But that was another story.

Hector knelt down to look for the cap under his bed.

"Hector!" his mother yelled again.

"In a minute, Mom!"

Sure enough, Hector's favorite Yankees cap was shoved way under the bed, where it had already collected plenty of dust.

I guess I've finally settled in, Hector thought, reaching under the bed to fish out the cap. *This room is just as messy as my old one!*

"There you are!" his mother said when Hector finally came down the stairs wearing his baseball hat. "The whole block is probably at the community garden already," she complained good-naturedly.

"Good. We'll make a big entrance, Mom."

"The Carreros *always* make a big entrance, Hector," Ruben piped up, grinning. "Do you need help carrying your present over?"

Hector nodded. Together he and his uncle went

down into the basement to get the bench that Hector had finished the day before.

"Yo, Hector!" somebody yelled as Hector, Ruben, and Maritza walked up to the garden.

Hector looked up. It was a hot, sunny afternoon, and lots of his neighbors were crowded into the Ellington Street Community Garden. Hector immediately spotted familiar faces—X and Miles, Brent Wolf, and Maritza's friends, Barbara and Sue, who were dancing to reggae music that blared from a portable CD player. A plume of white smoke from a barbecue drifted over the crowd.

"Hector!" X called his name again.

"Whatcha got there?" Miles chimed in.

"A present," Hector said. He put his end of the bench down for a minute so that he could point out a certain spot to Ruben.

"Looks good," Ruben said cheerfully. "Let's do it."

Together they carried the bench over to the shady spot under an apple tree and set it down.

"Perfect!" Hector pronounced.

"Check it out!" Sue said as she and Barbara came over. "Now we have a place to sit down and enjoy the flowers."

Hector looked around. He hadn't noticed until just now, but colorful flowers were blooming all around them.

He smiled. "I thought everyone would like having a bench in the garden."

"The neighborhood has been so nice to us," Maritza added. "Hector had the idea of giving something back."

X was walking around the bench, inspecting it. "Did you really make this thing?"

Hector nodded.

X let out a low whistle. "It's pretty sharp, Hector. How'd you learn to do something like this?"

Hector smiled at his mother. "My mom taught me," he said proudly. "Actually, she's taught me just about everything I know."

Hector thought he saw tears glimmering in his mother's eyes, but before he could tell for sure, Barbara held up her can of soda. "Here's to the Ellington Street Community Garden," she cheered. "And to our new neighbors, Hector and Maritza."

For the next few minutes, people came over and raved about Hector's bench. Even Marion Wolf couldn't find anything to complain about when she came over with a plateful of potato salad and hot dogs, and plopped herself down. "I've got to hand it to you, cookie," she told Hector. "This is the perfect spot for a hardworking baker like me to rest my weary legs."

X and Miles were sitting on the grass nearby, eating hot dogs. As Marion sat down, Hector saw X give Miles a sly grin. Hector knew something was up.

"So Mrs. Wolf," X called. "We were wondering about something."

"Yes?" She took a bite of her hot dog and peered at him.

"Is it a coincidence that your last name is Wolf . . ."

"And that your teeth are really sharp?" Miles finished.

Marion froze, her mouth full of food. For a second, Hector thought she was about to start yelling at them, or say something nasty back. Instead she calmly swallowed the bite of her hot dog, before she said anything. "Why, of course it's not a coincidence that my teeth are sharp," she said sweetly.

"It's not?" Miles winked at X, and the boys leaned in closer.

"Oh, no," Marion went on. Abruptly, her whole manner changed. "The better to eat you with!" she snarled. "Now leave me alone and let me eat my dinner in peace!"

X and Miles were so startled they didn't say a word. Hector laughed out loud as the two of them jumped up and hurried over to the other end of the garden, where Brent Wolf and some other kids were tossing a Frisbee back and forth.

Just then someone waved to Hector from behind the grill. "Hey, pickle boy."

Hector looked over at the grill, where José, from the deli, was barbecuing the hot dogs.

"Come on over and get some food," José yelled. "We don't have any pickles, but the dogs are pretty good—if I do say so myself."

Hector smiled. "I'm on my way," he called back. As he headed over, he could feel his stomach rumble. A hot dog would taste pretty good right now, he decided. Even without a pickle on the side.

As Hector waited for José to hand him a hot dog, he noticed an advertisement painted on the side of a tall building. The letters began to flicker and rearrange themselves.

Hector squinted to read the message from Ghostwriter.

I'm glad you've settled in, Hector . . . now you know that home is where the heart is.

130

Thanks, Ghostwriter, Hector thought as his friend faded away. *I think that's exactly what I figured out on my own.*

It had taken a while, but now Hector knew it was true. His heart—and his home—were on Ellington Street.